her characters where you find yourself thinking about them for days on end. I can't wait to see where this series is heading!"
—*Infinite Text*

Praise for Carrie Vaughn

On the Kitty Norville series

"Enough excitement, astonishment, pathos, and victory to satisfy any reader"
—Charlaine Harris, author of *Dead After Dark*

"[Vaughn] manages to combine outright thrills with an off-beat sense of humor and then mesh it with Kitty's dogged determination. The result—entertainment exemplified!"
—*Romantic Times*

"Fresh, hip, fantastic—a real treat!"
—L. A. Banks, author of the Vampire Huntress Legend series

"The only urban fantasy world where I want to read every book of the series."
—*Denver Post*

"Readers of Kim Harrison's 'Hollows' series and Jim Butcher's 'Dresden Files' will appreciate Kitty's sarcastic wit, ingenuity, and independence."
—*Library Journal*

ALSO BY THE AUTHOR

Introduction copyright © 2020 by Carrie Vaughn, LLC
Interior and cover design by Elizabeth Story
Cover art "Giving Velázquez a Hand" copyright © 2008 by Rebecca Harp

Tachyon Publications LLC
1459 18th Street #139
San Francisco, CA 94107
415.285.5615
www.tachyonpublications.com
tachyon@tachyonpublications.com

Series Editor: Jacob Weisman
Project Editor: Jill Roberts

Print ISBN 13: 978-1-61696-321-7
Digital ISBN: 978-1-61696-322-4

Printed in the United States by Versa Press, Inc.
First Edition: 2020
10 9 8 7 6 5 4 3 2 1

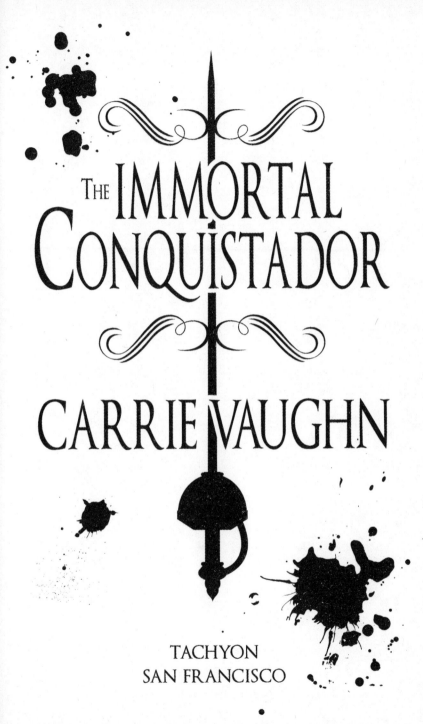

THE IMMORTAL CONQUISTADOR

CARRIE VAUGHN

TACHYON
SAN FRANCISCO

RICK SLUNG HIS BAG over his shoulder, descended the steel staircase from the plane to the tarmac, and set foot in Europe for the first time in five hundred years.

He paused a moment, taking a deep breath and wondering why this should feel so strange. It was only the ground, it was only the air. But this air did not have the crisp touch of mountain and plain that made Denver special. This air smelled of oil and urban sprawl, hummed with the underlying whine of aircraft engine. Orange sodium lights gave everything a burnt glow, and the night sky was all haze.

This was not home. Hadn't been for a long time. He'd left Avila when he was seventeen, such a small fraction of his life now. He barely remembered it. Now when he thought of home he thought of the desert, the American prairie, yucca and sagebrush standing fast in the wind, bright stars splashed across a wide night sky.

This ancient city Rome wasn't home. Everything about coming here felt unnatural. Maybe Kitty was right and he shouldn't have left Denver. Kitty the werewolf, the alpha of the Denver pack, blond and quintessentially modern, so earnest and unlikely, not at all suited to the world of monsters and yet there she was. Time was, Rick hadn't cared much for werewolves. Turned out he just hadn't met the right ones. Maybe he should have listened to her.

But he'd insisted. "I have to tell them what happened to Father Columban."

"Can't you call? Write a letter?" she'd said, some of her inner wolf coming through, as if she had a tail to wag even in her human form.

"I thought it best that I tell them in person."

"You think you have to replace him in the Order of Saint Lazarus of the Shadows."

Kitty hosted a talk radio show where she dispensed advice to the lovelorn and others with supernatural problems. She was good at it. Good at cutting through messes to the heart of the matter. Yes, when the vampire priest Columban had been destroyed, Ricardo had felt like something had been taken from the world and that he must replace it.

"You'll be back?" she had asked as he left.

He didn't know. He had lost so many friends. Her, he'd walked away from. He didn't know where he was going, who he was meeting with. He'd sent a message ahead to say he was coming. He was riding into the unknown and didn't know what would happen. But then, hadn't he spent most of his existence doing that?

He'd tried to explain all this to Kitty and was sure he'd failed.

He'd chartered a private jet to get here. Discovered that without really noticing he had become wealthy enough to be able to charter a private jet. Almost like he was a proper vampire, when for most of his existence he'd traveled by horseback and slept in whatever windowless closet he could beg an inn to rent him. But private jet was the only way to ensure arriving at night, with enough privacy to remain locked in the dark during daylight hours. However uneasy he felt about this journey, he needed to make it.

A black town car waited for him down the tarmac, which was typical and entirely expected. *These* were proper vampires, comfortable with wealth and power. The small, prim woman standing by the passenger door was simply but elegantly dressed in a dark skirt, cashmere shirt, and jacket. Almost monastic, but not quite. She gazed at him steadily, pressing neutrally painted lips together. She was a vampire, an old one, of Mediterranean heritage. This still told him very little about her.

He was not so elegant. He wore a T-shirt and jeans under his long overcoat and had not cared what he was wearing until now. It didn't matter, he decided. He was what he was.

"You're Ricardo?" she asked as he approached. She spoke with a British accent, one learned from the BBC news, so that didn't tell him anything about her history either.

"Rick is fine," he said. "You got my message?"

"We did. The Abbot is anxious to meet you." She opened the passenger door for him.

"The Abbot. The head of the Order of Saint Lazarus of the Shadows?" he asked. This was the thread that had brought him here. "Who is he?"

"You'll meet him."

"You're with the Order?"

"May I ask how you heard of us?"

"A vampire priest found me. Father Columban," he said. "I didn't believe him at first, when he told of an order of vampire monks. Then, I did. Did you know him?"

"Yes," she said after a moment. "Not well. He traveled much, and I stay here and help run the abbey."

"He was killed. I wanted to tell you—the Order—in person." Rick still wasn't sure what he was doing. Meeting the man had upended much of what he believed about the world, and about what he was. "He wanted to recruit me. But I'm still not sure I understand."

"You have a lot of questions. You'll have to ask the Abbot."

"And you are?"

She gazed at him coolly. "I am Portia."

A simple and elegant name to go with her look and manner. Also a Roman name. Could she be fifteen hundred years old or more? Could be.

"Pleased to meet you," he said. His own accent was as cultivated as hers, but pure, flat American. It made other vampires underestimate him—they assumed he was younger than he was.

"The night is wearing on," she said and gestured him into the car.

If Rick had still had a mortal heart, it would have been pounding. He should not be here, he should not have come. He ought to be home, he ought to be protecting his people in Denver—but he needed answers. A larger battle waited to be fought. Five hundred years he'd managed to keep out of the mess and tangle of vampire politics. Now here he was, walking into the middle of it. But he had information, which he hoped to trade for answers to questions of his own.

The vehicle's driver was not a vampire but had the smell of vampires all over him. A longtime servant, then. A loyal source of sustenance. These people would have an army of such servants, some of them tucked away in government, law enforcement. In the Church, even? Portia sat in the passenger seat, glanced back at him now and then, but otherwise left him alone to stare out the window.

They entered the city, and the road took them to a vista, a hundred lights set on ruins, cathedrals, ancient walls, the Colosseum, crammed together with a mix of other structures from across two thousand years. He'd never seen anything like it. If he'd still needed to breathe, his breath would have caught. He inhaled so he could speak.

"Wait. Can we pull over here? Can I look, just for a minute?"

Portia nodded to the driver, who pulled over at a likely spot, where a few trees framed the view. Rick immediately climbed out and just stood, looking. This was the weight of years made physical.

After a moment, Portia joined him. She looked at him, not the view. "Most of us who've been around as long as you have are more jaded than this."

He'd never been jaded, not once. He never tired of a good view. "This is my first time in Rome."

"As old as you are, and you've never been to Rome?" Portia said, laughing, a lilting sound, quickly cut off, as if she had not expected to make it. "What about Paris?"

"No."

"London? Cairo? Beijing? *Anywhere?* How is that possible?"

He shrugged. "Just never made the time." Which seemed

a ridiculous thing for one who was theoretically immortal to say. His fists closed. Yes, perhaps he should have made time. He should have come to see Rome, Paris. Should have traveled the world, even if he could only see such monuments lit up at night.

"Portia. Do you believe that vampires have souls?"

"What kind of question is that?"

"Saint Lazarus of the Shadows claims to be a holy order of vampires, which suggests that you all believe in God and the Church and the rest, which suggests that you believe we still have souls worth saving and protecting . . . and yet, I have met so many of our kind who are sure that we are damned. Who embrace being damned. So I wondered . . . is this order a religious order in truth, or a mask for something else? Are we all soulless monsters trying to repent, or children of God doing His will? Or something else entirely?"

"What does it matter?"

He had stayed alone, mostly, in out-of-the-way places, and he knew very little of the world of the truly old vampires. He'd liked it that way. When he did meet them, they always regarded him like Portia did now, like he was a child who had said something hilarious. But not knowing about their games and politics meant he did not have to play them. What was he getting himself into?

"You see," he continued, "I look out at a scene like this and feel so inspired, I have felt such hope and seen such beauty and experienced such kindness, despite all the grief and evil in the world. Would such feelings be possible if I did not have a soul? And yet I cannot go into a church. I'm a demon. A monster who drinks blood. I just wondered if you knew the answer to the paradox."

Portia stared at him a moment and said, "The Abbot very much wants to hear your story."

"I will be happy to tell him."

CONQUISTADOR
DE LA NOCHE

HIS LIFE was becoming a trail of blood.

Ricardo de Avila fired his crossbow at the crowd of natives. The bolt struck the chest of a Zuni warrior, a man no older than his own nineteen years. The native fell back, the dark of his blood splashing, along with dozens of others. The army's few arquebuses fired, the sulfur stink clouding the air. The horses danced, tearing up the grass and raising walls of dust. Between keeping control of his horse and trying to breathe, Ricardo could not winch back his crossbow for another shot.

Not that he needed to fire again. The general was already calling for a cease-fire, and the few remaining Zuni, running hard and shouting in their own language, were fleeing back to their city.

City. Rather, a few baked buildings clustered on the hillside. The expedition had become a farce. Cíbola did not exist— at least, not as it did in the stories the first hapless explorers had brought back. So many leagues of travel, wasted. Dead men and horses, wasted. The land itself was not even worth much. It had little water and was cut through with unforgiving mountains and canyons. The Spanish should turn around and leave it to the natives.

But the friars who traveled with Coronado were adamant. Even if they found no sign of treasure, it was their duty as Christians to save the souls of these poor heathens.

They had believed that Coronado would be a new Cortés, opening new lands and treasures for the glory of Spain. The New World was more vast than any in Europe had comprehended. Naturally they had assumed the entire continent held the same great riches Spain had found in Mexico. As quickly as Spain was eating through that treasure, it would need to find more.

Coronado tried to keep up a good face for his men. His armor remained brightly polished, gleaming in the harsh sun, and he sat a tall figure on his horse. But with the lack of good food, his face had become sunken, and when he looked across the *despoblado*, the bleak lands they would have to cross to reach the rumored Cities of Gold, the shine in his eyes revealed despair.

This expedition should have made the fortune of Ricardo, a third son of a minor nobleman. Now, though, he was thirsty, near to starving, and had just killed a boy who had come at him with nothing but a stone club. His dark beard had grown unkempt, his hair long and ratted. Sand had marred the finish of his helmet and cuirass. No amount of wealth seemed worth the price of this journey. Rather, the price he was paying had become so steep it would have taken streets paved with gold in truth to restore the balance.

What was left, then? When you had already paid too much in return for nothing?

Ricardo had sold himself for a mouthful of dust.

Ten years passed.

It was dark when Ricardo rode into the main plaza at Zacatecas. Lamps hung outside the church and governor's buildings, and the last of the market vendors had departed. A small caravan of a dozen horses and mules from the mine was picketed, awaiting stabling. The place was hot and dusty, though a cool wind from the mountains brought some refreshment. Ricardo stopped to water his horse and stretch his legs before making his way to the fort.

At the corner of the garrison road, a man stepped from the shadows to block his path. His horse snorted and planted its feet. Ricardo's night vision was good, but he had trouble making out the figure.

"Don Ricardo? I was told you were due to return today," the man said.

Ricardo recognized the voice, though it had been a long time since he'd heard it. "Diego?"

"Ah, you do remember!"

He'd met Diego in Mexico City, where they'd both listened to the stories of Cíbola and joined Coronado's expedition. Side by side they'd ridden those thousands of miles. They'd both grown skinny and shaggy, and, on their return, Diego had broken away from the party early to seek his own fortune. Ricardo hadn't seen him since.

"Where have you been? Come into the light, let me look at you!"

A lamp shone over the doorway on the brick building on the corner. Ricardo touched Diego's shoulder and urged him over. His old compatriot turned but didn't move from the spot. Ricardo squinted to see him better. Diego had not changed much in the last decade. If anything, he seemed more robust. He had a brightness to him, a sly smile, as if he had come into some fortune, discovering what the rest of them had failed to attain. His clothing, a leather doublet, breeches, and sturdy boots, were worn but well made. His hair and beard were well kept. He wore a gold ring in one ear and must have seemed dashing.

"You look very well, Diego," Ricardo said finally.

"And you look tired, my friend."

"Only because I have ridden fifteen miles today over hard country."

Diego grimaced. "Yes, playing courier for the garrisons along the road to Mexico City. How do you come to do such hard labor? It's not fit for one of your station."

Typical hidalgo attitude. Ricardo was used to the reaction. Smiling, he ducked his gaze. "The work suits me, and it won't be forever."

"Hoping to earn your way to a land grant? A silver mine of your very own, with a fine estancia and a well-bred girl from Spain to marry and give you many sons? So you can return to Spain a made man?" Diego spoke with a mocking edge.

"Isn't that the dream of us all?" Ricardo said, spreading his arms and making a joke of it. He really was that transparent, he supposed. Not dignified enough to lead the life of dissolute nobility like so many others of his class. Too proud and restless to wait for his fortune to find him. But the secret that he told no one was that he didn't want to leave and take his fortune back to Spain. He had come to love this land, the wide desert spaces, green valleys ringed by brown mountains, hot sun and cold nights. He wanted to be at home here.

Diego stepped close and put a hand on Ricardo's arm. "I have a better idea. A great opportunity. I was hoping to find you, because I know no one as honest and deserving as you."

The schemes to easy wealth were as common in this country as cactus and mountains. Ricardo was skeptical. "You have found some secret silver lode, is that it? You need someone in the government to push through the claim, and you'll give me a percentage."

Diego's smile thinned. "There is a village a day's ride away, deep in the western hills. The land is rich, and the natives are agreeable. A Franciscan has started a church there, but he needs men to lead. To make their mark upon the land." He pressed a folded square of paper into Ricardo's hand. A map, directions. "You are a good, honest man, Ricardo. Come and help us make a respectable town out of this place. And reap the rewards for doing so."

Such a village should have fallen under the governor of Zacatecas's jurisdiction. Ricardo would have heard of a priest in that region. Something wasn't right.

"I still dream of gold, Ricardo," Diego said. "Do you?"

"The Cities of Gold never existed."

"Not as a place. But as a symbol—this whole continent is a Cíbola, waiting for us to claim it."

"Just as we did the last time?" Ricardo said, scowling.

"But you'll come to this village. I'll wait for you."

Diego patted Ricardo on the shoulder, then slipped back into shadows. Ricardo didn't even hear him go. Thoughtful, worried, Ricardo made his way to the fort for the evening.

Ricardo followed Diego's map into the hills, not because he was lured by the promise of easy wealth, but because he wanted to discover what was wrong with the story.

The day was hot, and he traveled slowly, keeping to shade when he could and resting his horse by dismounting and climbing steep hills alongside it. He followed the ridge of mountains and hoped he had not lost the way.

Then he climbed a rise that opened into a valley, as Diego had described. A large pond, probably filled by a spring, provided water, and fruit trees grew thickly. A meadow covered the valley floor, and Ricardo could imagine sheep or goats grazing here, or crops growing. Much could be done with land like this.

A small village sat a hundred yards or so from the pond. The Franciscan's church was little more than a square cottage made of adobe brick, with a narrow tower. Wood and grass-thatched huts gathered around a dusty square.

No people were visible, no hearth fires burned. Not so much as a chicken scratched in the dirt. Four horses grazed in the meadow beyond the village. They glanced at Ricardo, then continued grazing. Riding into the village, he shouted a hail, which fell flat, as if the empty settlement absorbed sound. Dismounting, he left his horse by a trough that was dry.

A smarter man might have traveled with a troop of guards, or at least servants to ease his way. He had thought it easier to travel alone, learn what he could, and return as quickly as possible to report this to the governor. Now, the skin of his neck crawled, and he wondered if he might need a squad of soldiers before the day was through. He kept his hand on the hilt of his sword slung on his belt.

He went into the chapel.

The place might have been new. A few benches lined up before a simple altar. The wood was freshly cut, but they seemed to have been poorly built: rickety legs slotted into flat boards. Those seated would have to be careful if they didn't want to tumble to the dirt floor.

In front, the wood altar was bare, without even a cloth to cover it. No cross hung on the wall. The place had the sickly beeswax candle smell that imbued churches everywhere. At least that much was familiar. Nothing else was. He almost hoped to find signs of violence, because then he'd have some idea of what had happened here. But this . . . nothing . . . was inexplicable.

"¡Hola!" he called, cringing at his own raised voice. He had the urge to speak in a whisper, if at all.

A door in the back of the chapel opened. A small body in a gray robe looked out. "Who is it?"

A shiver crawled up Ricardo's spine, as if a ghost had stepped through the wall. He peered at the door, squinting, but the man was hidden in shadow.

"I am Captain Ricardo de Avila. Diego Ruiz asked me to come."

"Ah, yes! He told me of you." He straightened, shedding the air of suspicion. "Come inside, let us speak," the friar said, opening the door a little wider. Ricardo went to the back room as the friar indicated.

Like the chapel, this room had no windows. There was a table with a lit candle on it, several chairs, and a small, dirty portrait of the Blessed Virgin. There was a trapdoor in the floor, with a big iron ring to lift it. Ricardo wondered what was in the cellar.

"Take a seat. I have some wine," the friar said, going to a cabinet in the corner. "Would you like some?"

"Yes, please." Ricardo sat in the chair closest to the door.

The friar put one pewter cup on the table, poured from an earthenware jug, and indicated that Ricardo should take it. He took a sip; it was weak, sour. But his mouth was dry, and the liquid helped.

The friar didn't pour a drink for himself. Sitting on the opposite side of the table, he regarded Ricardo as if they were two men in a plaza tavern, not two dusty, weary colonials in a dark room lit by a candle. The man was pale, as if he spent all his time indoors. His hands, resting on the table, were thin, bony. Under his robes, his entire body might have been a skeleton. He had dark hair trimmed in a tonsure and a thin beard. He was a stereotype of a friar who had been relegated to the outer edges of the colony for too long.

"I am Fray Juan," the man said, spreading his hands. "And this is my village."

Ricardo couldn't hide his confusion. "Forgive me, Fray Juan, but Señor Ruiz told me this was a rich village. I expected to see farmers and shepherds at work. Women in the courtyard, weaving and grinding corn."

"Oh, but this is a prosperous village. You must take my word that appearances here aren't everything." His lips turned in a smile.

"Then what is going on here?" He had started to make guesses: Fray Juan was smuggling something through the village; he'd failed utterly at converting the natives and putting them to useful work and refused to admit it; or everyone had died of disease. But even then there ought to be some evidence. Bodies, graves, something.

Juan studied him with cold eyes, blue and hard as stones. Ricardo wanted to hold the stare, but something made him glance away. His heart was pounding. He wanted to flee.

The friar said, "You rode with Coronado, didn't you? The expedition to find Cíbola?"

Surviving that trip at all gave one a certain reputation. "Yes, I did. Along with Ruiz."

"Even if he hadn't told me I would have guessed. You have that look. A weariness, like nothing will ever surprise you again."

Ricardo chuckled. "Is that what it is? Something different than the usual cynicism?"

"I see that you are not a youth, but you are also not an old man. Not old enough to have the usual cynicism. Therefore, you've lived through something difficult. You're the right age for it."

A restless caballero wandering the northern provinces? He supposed there were a few of that kind. "You've changed the subject. Where is Ruiz?"

"He will be here," Fray Juan said, soothingly. "Captain, look at me for a moment." Ricardo did. Those eyes gleamed in the candlelight until they seemed to fill the room. The man was all eyes, shining organs in a face of shadows. "Stay here tonight. It's almost dusk, far too late to start back for Zacatecas. There are no other settlements within an hour's ride of here. Take the clean bed in the house next door, sleep tonight, and in the morning you'll see that all here is well."

They regarded one another, and Ricardo could never recall what passed through his mind during those moments. The Franciscan wouldn't lie to him, surely. So all must be well, despite his misgivings.

And Fray Juan was right; Ricardo must stay the night in any case. "When will Ruiz return?"

"Rest, Captain. He'll be at your side when you wake."

Ricardo found himself lulled by the friar's voice. The look in his eyes was very calming.

A moment later, he was sitting at the edge of a rope cot in a house so poorly made that he could see through the cracks in the walls. He didn't remember coming here. Had he been sleepwalking? Was he so weary that a trance had taken him? For all his miles of travel, that had never happened before. He hadn't eaten supper. He wondered how much of the night had passed.

His horse—he didn't remember caring for his horse; he'd left the animal tacked up near the trough. That jolted him to awareness. It was the first lesson of this vast country: Take care of your horse before yourself, because you'd need the animal if you hoped to survive the great distances between settlements.

Rushing outside, he found his bay mare grazing peacefully, chewing grass around its bit while dragging the reins. He caught the reins, removed the saddle and bridle, rubbed the animal down, and picketed it to a sturdy tree that had access to good grazing, since no cut hay or grain seemed available. He had found water in a small pond in the meadow.

Now that he was fully awake, studying the valley under the light of a three-quarters moon, Ricardo's suspicions renewed. This village was dead. He should have questioned the friar more forcefully about what had happened here. Nothing about this place felt right, and Fray Juan's calm assurances meant nothing.

Ricardo had reason to doubt the word of a man of God. It was a friar, another man of God, who had brought back the story of Cíbola, of a land covered in lush pastures and rich fields, of cities with wealth that made the Aztec Empire seem as dust. Coronado had believed those stories. They all had, until they had reached the edge of that vast and rocky wasteland to the north. They had whispered to each other, "*Is this it?*"

Ricardo de Avila would find Diego Ruiz and learn what had happened here.

The wind spoke strangely here, crackling through cottonwoods, skittering sand across the mud-patched walls of the buildings. In the first hut, where he'd been directed to stay, he found a lantern and lit it using his own flint. With the light, he examined the abandoned village.

If disease had struck, he'd have expected to see graves. If there had been an attack, a raid by some of the untamed native tribes in the mountains, he would have seen signs of violence: shattered pottery, interrupted chores. He'd have found bodies and carrion animals. But there was not so much as a drop of shed blood.

The huts were tidy, dirt floors swept and spread with straw, clay pots empty, water skins dry. The hearths were cold, the coals scattered. He found old bread, wrapped and moldy, and signs that mice had gnawed at sacks of musty grain.

In one of the huts, the blankets of a bed—little more than a straw mat in the corner—had been shoved away, the bed torn apart. It was the first sign of violence rather than abandonment. He picked up the blanket, thinking perhaps to find blood, some sure sign that ill had happened.

A cross dropped away from the folds of the cloth. It had been wrapped and hidden away, unable to protect its owner. The thought saddened him.

Perhaps the villagers had fled. He went out a little ways to try to find tracks, to determine what direction the villagers might have gone. Behind the church, he found a narrow path in the grass, like a shepherd might use leading sheep or goats into the hills. Ricardo followed it. He shuttered the lantern and allowed his vision to adjust to the moonlight, to better see into the distance.

He was partway across the valley, the village and its church a hundred paces behind him, when he saw a figure sitting at the foot of a juniper. A piece of clothing, the tail of a shirt perhaps, fluttered in the slight breeze that hushed through the valley.

"Hola," Ricardo called quietly. He got no answer and approached cautiously, hand on his sword.

The body of a child, a boy, lay against the tree. Telling his age was impossible because his body had desiccated. The skin was blackened and stretched over the bones. His face was gaunt, a leathery mask drawn over a skull, and chipped teeth grinned. Dark pits marked the eye sockets. It might have been part of the roots and branches. Ricardo might have walked right by it and not noticed, if not for the piece of rotted cloth that had moved.

The child had dried out, baked in the desert like pottery.

It looked like something ancient. Moreover, he could not tell what had killed it. Perhaps only hunger.

But his instincts told him something terrible had happened here. Fray Juan had to know something of what had killed this boy, and the entire village. Ricardo must find out what, then report this to the governor, then get word to the bishop in Mexico City. This land and its people must be brought under proper jurisdiction, if for no other reason than to protect them from people like Fray Juan.

He rushed back to the village, went to the church, and marched inside, shouting, "Fray Juan! Talk to me! Tell me what's happened here! Explain yourself!"

But no one answered. The chapel echoed, and no doors cracked open even a little to greet him. Softly now, he went through the strange decrepit chapel with no cross. The door to the friar's chamber was unlocked, but the room was empty. Not even a lamp was lit. The whole place seemed abandoned. He tried the trapdoor, lifting the iron ring—the door didn't move. Locked from the other side. He pounded on the door with his boot heel, a useless gesture. So, Fray Juan was hiding. No matter. He'd report to the governor, and Ricardo would return with a squad to burn the place to the ground to flush the man out. He wouldn't even wait until daylight to set out. He didn't want to sleep out the night in this haunted valley.

When he went to retrieve his horse, a man stood in his way.

In the moonlight, he was a shadow, but Ricardo could see the smile on his face: Diego Ruiz.

"Amigo," the man called, his voice light, amused. "You came. I wasn't sure you would."

"Diego, what's happened here? What's this about?"

"I told you, Ricardo. This land is rich. We are looking for men to help us reap those riches."

"I see nothing here but a wasted village," Ricardo said.

A new voice spoke, "You need to see with different eyes."

Ricardo turned, for the voice had come from behind him. He had not heard the man approach—he must have been hiding in one of the huts. Two more came with him, so that together the four circled Ricardo. He could not flee without confronting them. He turned, looking back and forth, trying to keep them all in view, unwilling to turn his back on any of them.

The four were very much like Ricardo—young men with pure Spanish features, wearing the clothing of gentlemen. Others who had swarmed to New Spain seeking fortunes, failing, and turning dissolute.

Ricardo drew his sword. One of them he could fight. But not four. Not when they had every advantage. How had they taken him by surprise? He should have heard them coming. "You've turned bandit. You think to recruit more to run wild with you? No, Diego. I have no reason to join you."

"You do not have a choice, amigo. I brought you here because we can use a man like you. Someone with connections."

Ricardo smiled wryly. "No one will pay my ransom."

They laughed, four caballeros in high spirits. "He thinks we'll ask for ransom," another said.

Ricardo swallowed back panic and remained calm. Whatever they planned for him, he would not make it easy. He'd fight.

"Señor, be at ease," spoke a third. "We won't hold you for ransom. We have a gift for you."

Ricardo chuckled. "I don't think so."

"Oh, yes. We'll bring you to serve our Master. It's a great honor."

"I will not. You all are evil."

The men did not argue.

They began to circle him, jackals moving close for a kill. They watched him, and their eyes were fire. He had to run, grab his horse and fly from here, warn the governor of this madness.

It was madness, for Diego lunged at him, weaponless, with nothing but outstretched arms and a wild leer. Ricardo held out his sword, blade level and unwavering, and Diego skewered himself on the point, through the gut. Ricardo expected him to cry out and fall. He expected to have to fight off the others for killing one of their own. But the other three laughed, and Diego kept smiling.

Ricardo held fast to the grip out of habit. Diego stood, arms spread, displaying what he'd done. No blood ran from the wound.

Ricardo pulled the sword back just as Diego wrenched himself off the blade. Still, the man didn't make a sound of pain. Didn't fall. Wasn't bothered at all. Ricardo resisted an urge to make the sign of the cross. Holy God, what was this?

"This is why we follow Fray Juan," Diego breathed. "Now, will you join us?"

Ricardo cried out a denial and charged again. These were demons, and he must flee. He crouched, grabbed a handful of dirt with his left hand. If he could not cut them, perhaps he could blind them. He flung it at the man behind him, who must be moving to attack. In the same motion he whirled, slashing with his blade, keeping some distance around him, enough to clear a space so he might reach his horse. He did not wait to see what happened, did not even think. Only acted. Like those old days of battle, fighting the natives with Coronado's company. That had been a strange, alien world. Like this.

He'd have sworn that his sword met flesh several times, but the men stood firm, unflinching. Ricardo might as well have been a child throwing a tantrum. They closed on him without effort.

Two grabbed his arms, bracing them straight out, holding him still. A third wrenched his sword from him. His captors bent back his arms until his back strained and presented him to Diego.

Ricardo struggled on principle, with no hope. His boots kicked at the dirt.

Diego regarded him with a look of amusement. He ran a gloved hand along Ricardo's chin, scraping his rough beard. Ricardo flinched back, but his captors held him steady. "You should know that you never had a chance against us. Perhaps you might take comfort in that fact."

"I take no comfort," Ricardo said, his words spitting.

"Good. You will have none." He opened his mouth. They all opened their mouths and came at him. They had the teeth of wild dogs. Of lions. Sharp teeth meant to rend flesh.

And they began to rend his.

He couldn't move. He'd been on a very long journey, and his limbs had turned to iron, chilled iron, that had been left out on a winter's night and was now rimed with frost. That image of himself—stiff flesh mounted on a skeleton of frosted iron, a red body fringed with white—struck him as oddly beautiful. It was an image of death, sunk into his bones. Memory recalled the ambush, arms clinging to him, breath leaving him, and the teeth. Demonic teeth, puncturing his flesh, draining his blood, his life. So he had died.

His next thought: What had he done to find himself relegated to hell? What else could this be? As in Dante's ninth circle, where the damned lay frozen solid in a lake, he was left to feel his body turning to frost, piece by piece. He tried to cry out, but he had no breath.

A hand rested on his forehead. If possible, it felt even colder, burning against Ricardo's skin like ice.

"Ricardo de Avila," the devil said. "You hear me, yes?"

Nothing would melt his body; he could not even nod. Struggling to speak, he felt his lips move, but nothing else.

"I will tell you what your life is now. You will never again see the daylight. To touch the sun is to burn. You are no longer a son of the Church. The holy cross and baptismal water are poison to you. From now on you are a creature of darkness. But these small sacrifices are nothing to the reward: from now on might be a very long time. You belong to me. You are my son. With your brothers, you will rule the night."

Ricardo choked on a breath that tasted stale, as if he had not drawn breath in a very long time. His mouth tasted sour. He said, "Is this hell?"

The devil sounded wry. "Not necessarily. In this life, you make or escape your own hell."

"Who are you?"

"You know me, Ricardo. I am Fray Juan, and I am your Master."

He shook his head. It wasn't that the numbness was fading. Rather, he was getting used to the cold. This body made of iron could move. "The governor . . . the king . . . I am loyal . . ."

"You are beyond them now. Open your eyes."

His lids creaked and cracked, like the skin was breaking, but he opened them.

He lay on a bed in a dark room. A few lanterns hung from hooks on the walls, casting circles of light and flickering shadows. Fray Juan sat at the edge of the bed. Arrayed elsewhere stood four men, fierce looking. The demons.

He felt trapped by the shadows that had invaded his dreams. They would destroy him. In a panic, he waited for the jolt of blood, the racing heartbeat that would drive him from the bed, allow him some chance of fighting and escaping. But he felt nothing. He put his hand around his neck and felt . . . nothing. No pulse. He wanted to sigh—but he had not drawn breath. He had only taken in enough air to speak. Now, the panic rose. This could not be, this was impossible, dead and yet not—

This was hell, and the demon with Fray Juan's shape was lying to him.

"Diego, bring the chalice," Juan said, not with the voice of a sympathetic confessor but with the edge of a commander.

A figure moved at the far end of the room. Even as Ricardo prayed, his ears strained to learn what was happening, his muscles tensed to defend himself.

"Hold him," Juan said, and hands took him, hauled him into a sitting position, and wrenched back his arms so he could not struggle. Another set of hands pinned his legs.

His eyes opened wide. Three of the caballeros braced him in a sitting position. The fourth—Diego, his old comrade Diego—brought forward a Eucharistic chalice made of pewter. He balanced it in a way that suggested it was full of liquid.

Ricardo drew back, pressing against his captors. "You wear Fray Juan's face, but you are not a priest. You can't do this, this is no time for communion."

Juan smiled, but that did not comfort. "This isn't what you think. What is wine, after the holy sacrament of communion?"

"The blood of Christ," Ricardo said.

"This is better," he said, taking the chalice from Diego.

Ricardo cried out. Tried to deny it. Turned his head, clamped shut his mouth. But Juan was ready for him, putting a hand over his face, digging his thumb between Ricardo's lips and prying open his jaw, as if trying to slide a bit in the mouth of a stubborn horse.

Juan was stronger than he looked. Ricardo screamed, a noise that came out breathless and wheezy. The chalice tipped against his lips.

The liquid smelled metallic. When it struck his tongue— a thick stream sliding down his throat, leaving a sticky trail—it tasted of wine and copper. With the taste of it came knowledge and instinct. Human blood, it could be no other. Even as his mind rebelled with the obscenity of it, his tongue reached for more, and his throat swallowed, greedy for the sustenance. Its thickness flowed like fire through his veins, and something in him rose up and sang in delight at its flavor.

The battle was no longer with the demons holding him

fast; it was with the demon rising up inside him. The creature that drank the blood and wanted more. A strange joy accompanied the feeling, a strength in his body he'd never felt before. Weariness, the aches of travel, fell away. He was reborn. He was invincible.

And it was false and wrong.

Roaring, he shoved at his captors, throwing himself out of their grasp. He batted away the chalice of blood. They lunged for him again, and Fray Juan cried, "No, let him go."

Ricardo pushed away from them. He pressed his back to the wall and couldn't go farther. He could smell the blood soaking into the blanket at his feet. He covered his face with his hands; he could smell the blood on his breath. He wiped his mouth but could still taste blood on his lips, as if it had soaked into his skin.

He had an urge to lick the drops of blood that had spilled onto his hand. He pressed his face harder and moaned, an expression of despair welling from him.

"You see what you are now?" Juan said, without sympathy. "You are the blood, and it will feed you through the centuries. You are deathless."

Ricardo stared at him. The blood flowing through his veins now was not his own. He could feel it warming his body, like sunlight on skin. Sunlight, which he would never see again, if Juan spoke true.

He drew a breath and said, "You are a devil."

"We all are."

"No! I don't know what you've done to me, but I am not one of you. I would rather die!"

Juan, a pale face in lamp-lit shadows, nodded to his four henchmen, who backed toward the ladder, which led to the trapdoor in the ceiling. One by one, they slipped out, watching Ricardo with glittering, knowing eyes. In a moment, Juan and Ricardo were alone.

"This is a new life," Juan said. "I know it is hard to accept. But remember: You have received a gift."

Then he, too, left the room. The door closed, and a bolt slid home.

Ricardo rushed to the door and tried to open it, rattling the handle. They had locked him in this hole. A damp chill from the walls pressed against him.

Ricardo lay back on the bed, hands resting on his chest. Eventually, the lamp's wick burned down. The light grew dim, until it was coin-sized, burnished gold, then vanished. Even in the dark, he could see the ceiling. He should not have been able to see anything in the pitch dark of this underground cell. But it was like he could feel the walls closing in. He waited for panic to take him. He waited for his heart to start racing. But he touched his ribs and could not feel his heart at all.

Hours had passed, though the time moved strangely. Even in the darkness, he could see shadows move across the ceiling, like stars arcing overhead. It was nighttime outside; he knew this in his bones. The night passed, the moon rose—past full now, waning. The way the air moved over his face told him this. Eventually, near dawn, he fell asleep.

He started awake when the trapdoor opened. His senses lurched and rolled, like a galleon in deep swells. He knew—

again, without looking, without seeing—that Juan and his four caballeros had returned. They had a warmth coursing through them, tinged with metal and rot, the scent of spilled blood. The thing inside him stirred, a hunger that cramped his heart instead of his belly. His mouth watered. He licked his lips, hoping for the taste of it.

Shutting his eyes, he turned his face away.

Another, a sixth being, entered the room with them. This one was different—warm, burning with heat, a flame in the dark, rich and beautiful. Alive. A heartbeat thudded, the footfalls of an army marching double time. A living person who was afraid.

"Ricardo. Look." Juan stood at the foot of the bed and raised a lantern.

Ricardo sat up, pressed against the wall. Two of the caballeros dragged between them a child, a boy seven or eight years old, very thin. The boy met his gaze with dark eyes, shining with fear. He whimpered, pulling back from the caballeros' grasp, but they held fast, their fingers digging into his skin.

Juan said, "This is one of the things you must learn, to take your place among my knights."

"No." But the new sensations, the new way of looking at the world, wanted this child. Wanted the warm blood that gave this child life. The caballeros hauled the boy forward, and Ricardo shook his head even as he reached for the child. "No, no—"

"You cannot stop it," Juan said.

The child screamed before Ricardo even touched him.

It was not him. It did not feel like his body. Something else moved his limbs and filled his mind with lust. His mouth closed over the artery in the child's neck as if he kissed his flesh. His teeth—he had sharp teeth now—tore the skin, and the blood flowed. The sensation of wet blood on tongue burned through him, wind and fire. His vision was gone, his mind was gone.

This was not him.

The blood, life-giving and terrible, filled him until he seemed likely to break out of his own skin. With enough blood, he could expand to fill the world. When they pulled the dead child away, he was drunk, insensible, his hands too weak to clutch at the body. He sat at the edge of the bed, his arms fallen to his sides, limp, his face turned up, ecstatic. He licked his lips with a blood-coated tongue. But it was not him. His eyes stung with tears. He could not open them to look at the horror he'd wrought.

He was not so cold anymore. Either he was used to it, or he could no longer feel at all. That was a possibility. That was most likely best. Even if this were not hell, what they had forced him to do would surely send him to hell when he did die.

If he did.

"It is incentive to live forever, is it not? Knowing what awaits you for these terrible crimes," Diego said with the smile of a wolf.

The friar had shown him what horrors this life held for him: he brought Ricardo a cross made of pressed gold. He kept it wrapped in silk, did not touch it himself. When Ricardo touched it, his skin burned. He could never touch a holy cross again. Holy water burned him the same. He could never go into a church. His baptism had been burned away from him. The Mother Church was poison to him now. God had rejected him.

But I do not reject God, Ricardo thought helplessly.

There were rewards. Juan kept calling them rewards. Mortal weapons could not kill him. Stabs and slashes with a sword, arquebus shot, falls, cracked bones, nothing would kill him. Only beheading, only a shaft of wood driven through the heart. Only the sun. He was immortal.

"You call this reward?" Ricardo had shouted. "To be forever shut out of God's heavenly kingdom?" Then he realized the truth: This was no tragedy for Juan, because the friar did not believe in God or heaven.

"Did you ever believe?" Ricardo whispered at him. "Before you became this thing, did you believe?"

Juan smiled. "Perhaps it is not that I didn't believe, but that I chose to join the other side of this war between heaven and hell."

Which was somehow even more awful.

Ricardo stood at the church wall one night. The moon waxed again, past new. Half a month, he'd been here. He didn't know what to do next—what he could do. They held him captive. He belonged with them now, because where else could he go?

They told him that the blood should taste sweet on his tongue, and it did. He still hated it.

Perhaps he looked for rescue. When he did not report to the governor, wouldn't a party come for him? A troop of soldiers would come to learn what had happened, and

Ricardo would intercept them, tell them the truth, and he would help them raze the church to the ground, destroy Juan and his caballeros.

And then they would destroy him, stake his heart, drag him into the sunlight for being one of them. So perhaps Ricardo wouldn't help them, but would hide.

Did he love existence more than life, then? More than heaven?

A jingling of bridles sounded behind him. Ricardo did not have to look; he sensed the four men approaching with the horses.

"Brother Ricardo, it's good you've finally come into the air. It's not good to be cooped up all the time."

"I'm not your brother," he said. His voice scratched, weak and out of practice. He had taken breathing for granted and had had to relearn how to speak.

Diego laughed. "We're all you have, now. You'll understand soon enough."

"He has lots of time to learn," said Octavio, one of the four demons who had once been men, who followed Juan. Rafael and Esteban were the others.

Diego said, "Ride with us. We hunt tonight, and you'll learn at our side." It was a command, not a request.

He followed, because what else could he do? Except perhaps stand in the open when the sun rose and let it burn him. But suicide was a sin. Even now, he believed it. He would show that he did not forsake God. He would ask for forgiveness every moment of his existence.

Diego seemed to be Fray Juan's lieutenant; he had been the first of them turned to this demon life, years ago now. That was why he looked no older than he had when they returned from Coronado's expedition.

He explained what they did here. "Each of us is as strong as a dozen men. But there are still those who know how to kill us. Those who would recognize certain signs and hunt us down."

"Who?" Ricardo asked. "What signs?"

"Secret members of the Inquisition for one. And what signs? Why, bodies. Too many bodies, all drained of blood!" They all laughed.

"New Spain is the perfect place for us. There are thousands of peasants dying by the score in mines, on campaigns, of disease. Out here on the borders, no one is even looking much. If a whole village dies, we say a plague struck. We take all the blood we need, and no one notices."

At the mention of blood, Ricardo's mouth watered. A hunger woke in him, like a creature writhing in his belly. Each time Diego said the word, his vision clouded. He shook himself to remain focused on the hills before them.

"I know how it is with you," Diego said. "We all went through this."

"Though the rest of us were perhaps not so holy to start with." Again they laughed, like young men riding to a night of revelry. That was what they looked like, what anyone who saw them would think. Not that anyone would see them out here. That was the point, to feed on as much blood as they wished without notice. A land of riches. Diego had not lied.

"It's eating away inside me," Ricardo said under his breath.

"The blood will still that," said Rafael. "The blood will keep you sane."

"Ironic," Ricardo said. "That you must become a monster to keep from going mad."

"Ha. I never thought of it like that," Diego said.

He is already mad, Ricardo thought.

They rode for hours. They could not go far—half the night, he thought. Then they must go back, to take shelter before dawn. He could feel the night slipping away in his bones. It was the same part of him that now called out for blood.

Rafael said, "The villages nearby know of us. They go to the hills to hide, but we find them. Look toward the hills, take the air into your lungs. You can sense them, can't you?"

The air smelled of dust, heat, sunlight that had baked into the land during the day and now rose into the chill of night, lost in the darkness. The breeze spoke of emptiness, of a vast plain where nothing larger than coyotes lived. When he turned toward the hills, though, he smelled something else. The warmth had a different flavor to it: life.

When they brought him the child, he had known what was there before he saw it. He could feel its life in the currents of the air; sense its heartbeat sending out ripples, like a stone tossed into a body of still water. A live person made a different mark on the world than one of these demons.

"Our kind are drawn to them, like iron to a lodestone," Diego said. "We cannot live without taking in the human blood we have lost. We are the wolves to their sheep."

"And now you hunt. Like wolves," said Ricardo.

"Yes. It's good sport."

"It's a thousand childhood nightmares come to life."

"More than that, even. Come on!"

He spurred his horse. Kicking dirt behind them, the other four followed.

It was just as Diego said: a hunt. The leader sent two of the caballeros to ascend the hill from a different direction. They flushed the villagers from their hiding places, where they lived in caves and lean-tos. Like animals, Ricardo could not help but think. Easier to hunt them, then, when one did not think of them as human. It was like facing the native tribes with Coronado all over again. The imbalance in strength between the two parties was laughable.

On horseback, Rafael and Octavio galloped across the hill, chasing a dozen people, many of them old, before them. Diego and Esteban had dismounted and tied their horses some distance away, waiting on foot for the prey to come to them.

Ricardo watched, and time slowed.

It was as if he played the scene out in his mind while someone told him the story. Diego moved too fast to see when he stepped in front of the path of a young man, grabbed his arm with one hand and took hold of his hair with the other. The boy didn't have time to scream. Diego held the body like a lover might, hand splayed across the boy's chest, holding him in place, while pulling back his head, exposing his neck. He bit, then sank with the boy to the ground while he drank. The boy didn't even thrash. He was like a stunned rabbit.

Each of the others chose prey and struck, plucking their chosen victims from the scattered, fleeing peasants. The creature lurking where Ricardo's heart used to be sang and longed to reach out and grab a rabbit for itself. As he watched, the scene changed, and it was not the caballeros who moved quickly, but the villagers who moved slowly. Ricardo had felt like this once in a swordfight. His own skills had advanced to a point where he had some proficiency, his mind was focused, and he knew with what seemed like supernatural prescience what his opponent was going to do. He parried every attack with ease, as if he watched from outside himself.

This was the same.

It was not himself but the unholy monster within who stepped aside as a woman ran past him, then slipped into place behind her and took hold of her shoulders, moving like the shadow of a bird in flight across the land.

Jerked off her feet by his hold on her, she screamed and fell against him, thrashing, panicked, like an animal in a snare. He held her, embraced her against his body to still her, and touched her face. The coiled hunger within him gave him power. As he ran his finger down her cheek and closed his hand against her face, she quieted, stilled, went limp in his grasp. Her heartbeat slowed. He could take her, drink her easily, without struggle. This was better, wasn't it? Would he have this power if this wasn't what he was meant to do? She was young, almost a girl, her skin firm and unlined, lips full, her eyes bright. He could have her in all ways, strip her, lie with her, and he could make her want it, make her open to him in a way their Catholic religion would never allow, even in marriage. In the ghostly moonlight, she was beautiful, and she belonged to him. He laid her on the ground. She clutched his hand, and confusion showed in her eyes.

He couldn't do it. He sat with her as though she were

his ill sister, holding her hand, brushing damp hair from her young face. The creature inside him thrashed and begged to devour her. Ricardo felt the needle-sharp teeth inside his mouth. And he turned his gaze inward, shutting it all away.

I am not this creature. I am a child of God. Still, a child of God, like her. And the night is dangerous.

Quickly, he made her sit up. He laid his hand on her forehead and whispered, "Wake up. You must run." She stared at him blankly, groggily. He slapped her cheek. She didn't even flinch. "Wake up, please. You must wake up!"

Her gaze focused. At last she heard him. Perhaps she didn't understand Spanish. But then, which of a dozen native dialects would she understand?

Fine, he thought. He didn't need language to tell her to run. He bared his teeth—the sharp fangs ripe for feeding, wet with the saliva of hunger—and hissed at her. "Run!"

She gasped, scrambled to her feet, and ran across the hillside and into shadow.

Just in time. The world shifted, the action around him sped up and slowed as it needed to, and all appeared normal again. A still night lit by a waxing moon, quiet unto death.

The caballeros surrounded him. Ricardo could sense the blood on their breaths, and his belly rumbled with hunger. He bowed his head, content with the hunger, with the choice he had made.

They could probably smell on him the scent of resignation.

"Brother Ricardo," Diego said. "Aren't you hungry? Were the pickings not easy enough for you?"

"I'm not your brother," Ricardo said.

Diego laughed, but nervously. "Don't starve yourself to spite us," he said.

"Don't flatter yourself," Ricardo said. "I don't starve myself for you."

The four demons looked down on him, where he sat in the dust, content. They would kill him, and that was all right. The demon they had given him screeched and complained. Ricardo sat rigid, keeping it trapped, refusing to give it voice.

"You're not strong enough to survive this," Diego said. "You don't have the will to refuse the call of our kind."

At this, Ricardo looked at him with a hard gaze. Unbelievably, Diego took a step back.

"I was one of the hundred who returned to Mexico City with Coronado. Don't tell me about my will."

To his left, a branch snapped as Octavio broke a twisting limb off a nearby shrub. "Diego, I will finish him. Turning him was a mistake."

"Yes," Diego said. "But we didn't know that."

"We'll leave him. Leave him here and let the sunlight take him," said Rafael.

Diego watched him with the air of a man trying to solve a riddle. "The Master wants to keep him. The governor will listen to him, and he will keep us safe. He must live. Captain Ricardo de Avila, you must accept what you are, let the creature have its will."

Ricardo smiled. "I am a loyal subject of Spain and a child of God who has been saddled with a particularly troublesome burden."

Diego looked at Octavio. Ricardo was ready for them.

Together, the thing coiled inside him and his honor as a man of Spain rose up to defend if not his life, then his existence. Octavio made an inhuman leap that crossed the distance between them, faster than eye could see. The perception that made time and the world around Ricardo seem strange and move thickly, like melting wax, served him now. For all Octavio's speed, Ricardo saw him and wasn't there when his enemy struck.

He could learn to revel in this newfound power.

Ricardo longed for a sword in his hand, no matter that steel would do no good against these opponents. He would have to beat them with wood through the heart. Octavio held the torn branch, one end jagged like a dagger. The other three ranged around him, ready to cut off his escape, and a wave of dizziness blurred Ricardo's vision for a moment. Despair and hunger. If he'd taken blood, he would have more power—maybe enough to fight them all. As it was, he could not fight all four of them. Not if they meant to kill him.

He ran. They reached for him, but with flight his only concern, he drew on that devilish power. *Make me like shadow,* he thought.

The world became a blur, and he was smoke traveling across it. Nothing but air, moving faster than wind. He felt their hands brush his doublet as he passed. But they did not catch hold of him.

He found a cave. Villagers might have hidden here once. Ricardo found the burned remains of a campfire, some scraps of food, and an old blanket that had been abandoned. The back of the cave was narrow and ran deep within the hillside. It would always be dark, and he could stay there, safe from sunlight.

But would they come after him?

They could not tolerate rivals. Animal, demon, or men fallen beyond the point of redemption, they had claimed this territory as their own. He had rebuffed their brotherhood, so now he was an invader. They would come for him.

Ricardo put the blanket over a narrow crag in the rock, deep in the cave. The light of dawn approached. As he lay down in the darkness, he congratulated himself on surviving the night.

He fell asleep wondering how he would survive the next.

At dusk, he hurried over the hillside, gathering fallen sticks, stripping trees of the sturdiest branches he could find, and using chipped stones he had found in the cave to sharpen the ends into points. It was slow going, and he was weak. Lack of blood had sapped his strength. His skin was clammy, pale, more and more resembling a dead man's. *I am a walking corpse,* he thought and laughed. He had thought that once before, while crossing the northern *despoblado* with Coronado.

Ricardo had to believe he was not dead, that he would not die. He was fighting for a much nobler cause than the one that had driven him north ten years ago. He'd made that journey for riches and glory. Now he was fighting to return to God. He was fighting for his soul. But without blood, he couldn't fight at all.

"Señor?" a woman's voice called, hesitating.

Ricardo turned, startled. It was a sign of his weakness that he had not heard her approach. Now that he saw her, the scent of her blood and the nearness of her pounding heart washed over him, filling him like a glass of strong wine. His mind swam in it, and the demon screeched for her blood. Ricardo gripped the branch in his hand, willing the monster to be silent.

The mestiza woman wore a poor dress and a ragged shawl over her head. Her hair wasn't tossed and tangled in flight tonight, but he recognized her. She was the one he'd let go.

"You," he breathed, and discovered that he loved her, wildly and passionately, with the instant devotion of a drunk man. He had saved her life, and so he loved her.

She kept her gaze lowered. "I hoped to find you. To thank you." She spoke Spanish with a thick accent.

"You shouldn't have come back," he said. "My will isn't strong tonight."

She nodded at his roughly carved stake. "You fight the others? The wolves of the night?"

He chuckled, not liking the tone of despair in the sound. "I'll try."

"But you are one of them."

"No. Like them, but not one of them."

She knelt on the ground and drew a clay mug from her pouch. She also produced a knife. She moved quickly, as if she feared she might change her mind, and before Ricardo could stop her, she drew the knife across her forearm. She hissed a breath.

He reached for her. "No!"

Massaging her forearm, encouraging the flow of blood, she held the wound over the mug. The blood ran in a thin stream for several long minutes. Then, just as quickly, she took a clean piece of linen and wrapped her arm tightly.

The knife disappeared back in the pouch. She glanced at him. He could only stare back, dumbfounded.

She moved the cup of blood toward him. "A gift," she said. "Stop them, then leave us alone. Please?"

"Yes. I will."

"Thank you."

She turned and ran.

The blood was still warm when it slipped down his throat. His mind expanded with the taste of it. He no longer felt drunk; on the contrary, he felt clear, powerful. He could count the stars wheeling above him. The heat of young life filled him, no matter if it was borrowed. And he could survive without killing. That gave him hope.

He scraped the inside of the cup with his finger and sucked the film of blood off his skin, unwilling to waste a drop. After tucking the mug in a safe place, he climbed to his hiding place over the cave and waited. He had finished his preparations in time.

They came like the Four Horsemen of Revelations, riders bringing death, armed with spears. They weren't going to toy with him. They were here to correct a mistake. *Let them come,* he thought. Let them see his will to fight.

They pulled to a stop at the base of the hill, within sight of the cave's mouth. The horses steamed with sweat. They must have galloped most of the way from the village.

Diego and the others dismounted. "Ricardo! We have come for you! Fray Juan wants you to return to him, where you belong!"

Ricardo could smell the lie on him. He could see it in the

spears they carried, wooden shafts with sharpened ends. The other three dismounted and moved to flank the cave, so nothing could escape from it.

Octavio stepped, then paused, looking at the ground. Ricardo clenched fistfuls of grass in anticipation. Another step, just one more. But how much could Octavio sense of what lay before him?

"Diego? There's something wrong—" Octavio said, and leaned forward. With the extra weight, the ground under him collapsed. A thin mat of grass had hidden the pit underneath.

Almost, Octavio escaped. He twisted, making an inhuman grab at earth behind him. He seemed to hover, suspended in his moment of desperation. But he was not light enough, not fast enough, to overcome his surprise at falling, and he landed, impaled on the half-dozen stakes driven into the bottom of the pit. He didn't even scream.

"Damn!" Diego looked into the pit, an expression of fury marring his features.

Ricardo stood and hurled one of his makeshift spears at the remaining riders. He put all the strength and speed of his newfound power, of the gift of the woman's blood, into it, and the spear sang through the air like an arrow. He never should have been able to throw a weapon so strong, so true.

This curse had to be good for something, or why would people like Juan and Diego revel in it? He would not revel. But he would use it. The bloodthirsty demon in him reveled in this hunt and lent him strength. They would come to an understanding. Ricardo would use the strength—but for his own purpose.

The spear landed in Rafael's chest, knocking him flat to the ground. He clutched at the shaft, writhing, teeth bared and hissing in what might have been anger or agony. Then, he went limp. His skin tightened, wrinkling, drying out, until the sunken cavities of his skull were visible under his face. His clothes drooped over a desiccated body. He looked like a corpse years in the grave. That was how long ago he'd died, Ricardo thought. He had been living as a beast for years. But now perhaps he was at peace.

Diego and Esteban were both flying up the hill toward him. Almost literally, with the speed of deer, barely touching earth. Ricardo took up another spear. This would be like fighting with a sword, a battle he understood a little better. They had their own spears ready.

He thrust at the first to reach him, Esteban, who parried easily and came at him, ferocious, teeth bared, fangs showing. Ricardo stumbled back, losing ground, but braced the spear as his defense. Esteban couldn't get through to him. But then there was Diego, who came at Ricardo from behind. Ricardo sensed him there but could do nothing.

Diego braced his spear across Ricardo's neck and dragged him back. Reflexively, Ricardo dropped his weapon and choked against the pressure on his throat, a memory of the old reaction he should have had. But now, he had no breath to cut off. The pressure meant nothing. Ricardo fell, letting his head snap back from under the bar, and his weight dropped him out of Diego's grip. Another demonic movement. But he would not survive this fight as a human.

Esteban came at him with his spear, ready to pin him to the ground. Ricardo rolled and did not stop when he was clear. *I am mist, I am speed.* He spun and wrenched the spear from Esteban's grip. Esteban was charging one way and couldn't resist the force of Ricardo's movement in another direction. Even then, Ricardo didn't stop. He slipped behind Esteban, who had pivoted with equal speed and grace to face him. But he had no weapon, and Ricardo did. He speared the third of the demons through his dead heart. Another desiccated corpse collapsed at his feet.

Ricardo stared at Diego, who stood by, watching.

"I was right to want you as one of Fray Juan's caballeros," Diego said. "You are very strong. You have the heart to control the power."

"Fray Juan is a monster."

"But Ricardo, New Spain is filled with monsters. We both know that."

Screaming, Ricardo charged him. Diego let him run against him, and they both toppled to the ground, wrestling.

How did one defeat a man who was already dead? Who moved by demonic forces of blood? Ricardo closed his hands around the man's throat, but Diego only laughed silently. He did not breathe—choking did no good. He tried to beat the man, pound his head into the ground, but Diego's strength was effortless, unyielding. He might as well wrestle a bear.

Diego must have grown tired of Ricardo's flailing, because he finally hit him, and Ricardo flew, tumbling down the hill, away from his dropped weapons. Diego loomed over him now, with the advantage of high ground.

Ricardo made himself keep rolling. Time slowed, and he knew what would happen—at least what might happen. So he slid all the way to the bottom of the hill and waited. He wasn't breathing hard—he wasn't breathing at all. He hadn't broken a sweat. He was as calm as still water. But Diego didn't have to know that.

The smart thing for Diego to do would be to drive a spear through his chest. But Ricardo thought Diego would gloat. He'd pick Ricardo up, laugh in his face one more time, before tossing him aside and stabbing him. Ricardo waited for this to happen, ready for it.

But he'd also be ready to dodge if Diego surprised him and went for a quick kill.

"Ricardo! You're more than a fool. You're an idealist," Diego said, making his way down the hill, sauntering like a man with an annoying chore at hand.

God, give me strength, Ricardo prayed, not knowing if God would listen to one such as him. Not caring. The prayer focused him.

He struggled to get up, as if he were weak, powerless, starving. Let Diego think he had all the power. He flailed like a beetle trapped on his back, while Diego leaned down, twisted his hands in the fabric of his doublet, and hauled him to his feet.

Then Ricardo took hold of the man's wrists and dragged him toward the hole that had swallowed Octavio.

Diego seemed not to realize what was happening at first. His eyes went wide, and he actually let go of Ricardo, which was more than Ricardo had hoped for. Using Diego's own arms for leverage, he swung the man and let go. Diego was already at the edge of the pit, and like Octavio he made an effort to avoid the fall. But with the grace of a drifting leaf, he sank.

Ricardo stood on the edge and watched the body, stuck on the stakes on top of Octavio, turn to a dried husk.

He gathered up their horses and rode back to the church, torn between wanting to move and worrying about breaking the horses down. They had already made this trip once, and they were mortal. He rode both as quickly and slowly as he dared, and when he reached the village, the sky had paled. He could feel the rising sun within his bones.

Rushing, he unsaddled the horses and set them loose in the pasture. He would need resources, when he started his new life, and they were worth something, even in the dark of night.

He had only moments left to find Juan. Striding through the chapel, he hid a spear along the length of his leg.

"Juan! Bastard! Come show yourself!"

The friar was waiting in the back room where Ricardo had first spoken with him, a respectable if bedraggled servant of God hunched over his desk, watching the world with a furtive gaze.

"I felt it when you killed them," the friar said in a husky voice. "They were my children, part of me—I felt the light of their minds go out."

Don't let him speak. Ricardo's own power recognized the force behind the words, the connection that bound them together. His power flowed from the other.

Ricardo started to lunge, but the friar held up a hand and said, "No!" The younger man stopped, spear upraised, face in a snarl, an allegorical picture of war.

Fray Juan smiled. "Understand, you are mine. You will serve me as my caballeros served me. You cannot stop it." The Master had a toothy, wicked smile.

Ricardo closed his eyes. He'd fought for nothing, all these years and nothing to show for it but a curse. He was not even master of his fate.

Free will was part of God's plan. What better way to damn the sinful than to let them choose sin over righteousness? But he had not chosen this. Had he? Had something in his past directed him to this moment? To this curse?

Then couldn't he choose to walk away from this path?

He started to pray out loud, all the prayers he knew. *Pater Noster, Ave Maria*, even passages of Psalms, what he could remember.

The friar stared back at him. His lips trembled. "You should not be able to speak those words," Juan said. "You are a demon. One of Satan's pawns. He is our father. The holy words should burn your tongue."

"Then you believe the tales of the Inquisition? I don't think I do. Come, Juan, pray with me." Louder now, he spoke again, and still Juan trembled at the words.

"They're only words, Padre! Why can't you speak them?" Ricardo shouted, then started the prayers again.

The hold on his body broke. He had been balanced, poised for the strike, and now he plunged forward, his spear leading, and drove it into the friar's chest. Juan tumbled back in his chair, Ricardo standing over him, still leaning on the spear though it wouldn't go farther. Juan didn't make a sound.

Juan's skin turned gray. It didn't simply dry into hard leather; it turned to dust, crumbling away, his cassock collapsing around him. A corpse decayed by decades or centuries.

Ricardo backed away from the dust. He dropped the

spear. His knees gave out then, and he folded to the floor, where he curled up on his side and let the sleep of daylight overcome him.

Rumor said that the small estancia had once been a mission, but that the friar who ran it went mad and fled to the hills, never to be seen again. A young hidalgo now occupied the place, turning it into a quiet manor that bred and raised sheep for wool and mutton. The peasants who lived and worked there were quiet and seemed happy. The governor said that the place was a model from which all estancias ought to learn.

The hidalgo himself was a strange, mysterious man, seldom seen in society. Of course, all the lords in New Spain with daughters had an interest in getting to know him, for he was not only successful but unmarried. But the man refused all such overtures.

It was said that Don Ricardo had ridden north with Coronado. Of course, that rumor had to be false, because everyone knew Ricardo was a man in the prime of his life, and Coronado's expedition to find Cíbola rode out fifty years ago.

But such wild rumors will grow up around a gentleman who only leaves his house at night.

EL HIDALGO
DE LA NOCHE

CHRISTMAS NIGHT, Don Ricardo de Avila leaned against the outside wall of the newly expanded San Agustín church at Zacatecas and listened to the choir. He pressed his ear to the stone as if that would allow him to better hear the voices mixed in ethereal harmonies raised to the heavens. Closing his eyes, he bowed his head and sent his own prayers up with the song. He did not know if God would listen to him, but he prayed anyway.

The new church was magnificent, with towering walls and a great dome, but the choir was harder to hear through the stone than the clay bricks of the old. He felt farther from God than ever.

If he could have gone inside the consecrated church to hear Mass, he would have. But he could not, so he stood here and hoped it was enough. Every Christmas when the weather was fair and there were no other obstacles, he came to hear the choir and pray to the stars. Perhaps it was a risk. Perhaps one of these years he would be caught outside at dawn, or someone in the town would discover that he was a monster and destroy him. Some years he considered not coming, even when the sky was clear and the road was easy. But then he'd decide that no, it was Christmas, he should go and hear Mass, even if only as a whisper through stone walls. Every time, when he heard the voices converging in such heartfelt praise that his eyes watered with joy and pain, he was glad he came. If he could put those voices in a bottle and carry them with him forever, the world would not seem so ill a place.

He left before the Mass ended, before congregants streamed out of the church. He wouldn't have to speak to anyone, to explain why he didn't go inside like a good Christian man. He adjusted his cloak more firmly over his shoulders out of habit, not because he was cold. He was never cold anymore.

He was halfway to the respectable inn—with shutters and substantial curtains over the windows—where he had taken a room for the day, when a prickling feeling on the back of his neck stopped him. This wasn't cold, it wasn't fear. It pressed against him from the outside rather than welling up from within. This wasn't even the feeling you got while walking alone at night, wondering if a thief trailed you.

To add to the strangeness—he had felt this before, an alien presence like a hand on his shoulder. But that had been almost a hundred years ago. Had Fray Juan and his demons returned? Impossible. Ricardo had destroyed them, turned them to dust when he drove stakes through all their hearts. They could not return. He was all that was left of their evil, and every day he tried to atone, determined to prove that his good true nature still remained. That he still had his soul.

His mind rather than his eyes turned toward the impossible presence he felt, and he moved to face the danger.

A very fine gentleman stepped out of the shadows. He wore brocade slops and doublet in deep blue and gold, an intricate lace collar, and a plumed hat. He smiled through a neatly trimmed beard and mustache and rested his hand on the hilt of a rapier hanging on his belt. With his leg forward and ankle turned, his shoulders straight, he might have been a painting come to life. Ricardo had a sword under his cloak but he didn't reach for it. It wouldn't do much good. Now, what did this monster want?

"Buenas noches," the fine gentleman said.

"Buenas noches," Ricardo agreed, making a slight bow.

The man's amusement was a mask. The tension of his body, his hand on the sword, said that he was at least uncertain, if not worried. "I confess, my friend, I did not expect to find one such as you out on this fine night."

"Nor I you," Ricardo said. He was not as well dressed as the man—his doublet was only wool, though fine wool, and his boots were worn. But he was home, and that gave him some advantage. He could be at ease and thereby show some little superiority. "Please pardon me, but I am very surprised to see you. I have many questions."

The gentleman had no heartbeat. The air around him seemed chilled, and he moved with devilish calm. One of the demons for certain.

The demon's uncertainty grew. "As do I. Señor, you seem gentlemanly, so do not take this the wrong way, but you— you should not be here."

"This has been my home for a very long time."

The man's consternation grew. "I believe that isn't possible."

Ricardo chuckled; he couldn't help it. "As you see, it is. I have said something to upset you—perhaps we should go to some quiet place where we can talk? We can share our stories."

"I ask again, who are you?" The stranger would draw the sword in a moment.

"I am Don Ricardo de Avila, sir."

"And what Master do you serve?"

"I—I do not understand."

"It is a simple question. You do not appear powerful enough to be a Master yourself, you have no offspring you have made attending you. Are you saying that you are here alone?"

Wary, Ricardo recognized the pieces of a puzzle but could not fit them together. "Yes, that is just what I'm saying."

The gentleman marched forward, and Ricardo used all his will to stand his ground, not to reach for his sword. That chill he felt in the back of his mind was focused now— it was a sixth sense telling what this man was. He knew not to look into the man's eyes—his gaze held power. He knew, somehow, that the gentleman was not nearly as old as Fray Juan had been. Face to face they stood, studying one another, heedless that others now passed on the street, folk leaving the cathedral and calling greetings to one another.

He merely studied Ricardo and did not strike. His hands relaxed. "Yes, perhaps we should go somewhere to talk. You know a place?"

"You still have not told me who you are."

"I am Eduardo Montes y Contada of the House Catalina."

"And what is House Catalina?"

"Do you know nothing?"

"It would seem not." He did not appreciate being made to feel like a child by this man. But perhaps he was a child among demons.

"Then let us go inside to try to solve this mystery, hm?"

Don Eduardo kept looking warily at Ricardo as if he expected some kind of trick.

Ricardo's inn was small—one had to be a friend, or a friend of a friend, of the proprietor to stay here. Ricardo had known the man's grandfather. There was a small common room and hearth for guests.

At the door, Eduardo hesitated, his thin smile more mask-like than ever. "This is a tavern, you said? A public place?"

Ricardo had already opened the door and stood on the threshold. The other man held back, eyeing the space before him warily. He was so bold in every other way, why didn't he stride forward?

"It's small, not so crowded and noisy as others. I like it. Mostly, it is the innkeeper's friends who gather."

"So it is his home?" He sounded unhappy.

"It feels so sometimes, I suppose."

Just then the proprietor's daughter, Marie, saw him and waved. "Ricardo! Come in, come in, and bring your friend! You are both welcome!"

Eduardo relaxed and stepped forward as if a wall had vanished before him. His discomfort was gone, and Ricardo studied him.

"Pardon my forwardness," Ricardo asked carefully. "But what was wrong just then? You seemed unsure of the place."

Eduardo spoke softly as they made their way to a table in the corner. "Have you never tried to enter a home where you were not welcome?"

"No, I never have," said Ricardo.

The other demon seemed amused. "Some places, we need an invitation to enter. Do you not know this?"

"No," Ricardo said wonderingly.

"But how have you lived all this time? You know nothing!"

Apparently, Ricardo didn't even know how little he knew. "And that is why we are talking, yes?"

The common room was brightly lit and merry this night. Not everyone had gone to Mass, but they still celebrated with food and drink, singing and spilling wine, throwing more fuel on the fire. Ricardo felt very much the outsider here. He could look on, he could smile and pretend to take part. He had been like this once, newly arrived to a Mexico that was wild and full of adventure.

Marie brought over cups of the mulled wine that everyone was drinking. She'd surely think it odd when it was clear the two men hadn't touched the drinks. But for now, they were part of the disguise. They were just two men come out of the cold.

Eduardo gazed around him with an unmistakable hunger. Likely, *he* did not feel like an outsider. He looked like a hunter.

"I see why you like this place," Eduardo said. Ricardo didn't think so but didn't argue.

"You are new to this country, yes?" Ricardo asked. "You sailed from Spain?"

"Yes. A few years ago now. We settled in Mexico City and now I'm having a bit of a look around the rest of our new country." He looked Ricardo up and down. "I didn't expect to find one such as you."

"So you said."

"When did you arrive here?"

"A hundred years ago."

"But . . . no one was here a hundred years ago."

In fact, there'd been a whole native civilization here, and a thousand villages besides. But that wasn't what Eduardo was talking about. "I was one of Coronado's men."

Eduardo was perhaps the only man in the room who would believe this tale. He gave a short, brief laugh. "Really? Hm. Mistress Catalina must meet you. You . . . are extraordinary, sir. If I may say so."

"Gracias—I think."

Eduardo leaned back in his chair, gazing haughtily around the room, no more willing to look Ricardo in the eyes than Ricardo was to look in his. Oh yes, they would not be dueling with rapiers tonight. Not when steel wouldn't kill either one of them.

"What is the girl's name? Call her over." He tipped his chin toward Marie, who was wiping down a table at the far corner.

Rick raised his hand and caught Marie's gaze. She was a mestiza—her father had married a native woman. Marie turned heads wherever she went, with her bright eyes and silky black hair. She came right over.

"Yes, sirs? What do you like?"

"Come here and sit by me for a moment," Eduardo said,

catching the young woman's gaze. Her smile fell as the man took hold of her wrist and pulled her onto the bench beside him. Stroking the back of her hand, he murmured softly, and she sank willingly, powerlessly.

Eduardo raised the woman's hand to his lips, almost as if he meant to kiss her in some gentle romantic gesture. Instead, he turned the hand over, parted his lips, and closed his mouth over the inside of her wrist.

Ricardo's gut gave a jackrabbit leap, and he reached across the table for the demon's sleeve. "What are you doing?" he demanded.

Eduardo eyed him, swallowing a mouthful of blood before licking his teeth. "This is an inn. I will have drink."

"Let her go," Ricardo said.

"What do you care about her?" He licked a stray drop of blood from the wound. Marie's head slumped forward as if she slept. She was alive, her blood still pulsed; he hadn't drunk very much of her.

"She isn't yours."

"Is she yours?"

"She's nobody's but her own. You can't treat her like some rabbit you've caught in a snare—"

"But Don Ricardo, that's exactly what she is to us. What all these people are."

"All of them? I notice that you set your gaze upon the young woman, and not upon any of the strong men here."

"Then what do you harvest? Where do you find your drink?"

"I ask," he said. He didn't know how to explain it. When he learned he didn't need to kill to survive—well, he didn't. He asked. It had worked so far.

"You ask," Eduardo repeated. "Hmm."

Marie started to wake up from the trance Eduardo had put her in. He patted her hand; she might have fainted.

"You must be very tired, señorita. You fell asleep for a moment. You should go have a drink and rest," he said.

"Yes. Oh, I'm very sorry." She smiled apologetically at Ricardo, as if she were the one who ought to feel ashamed.

"Quite all right."

She fled.

Eduardo, face flush with new blood, regarded Ricardo. "You have been in this country all alone for a hundred years? You ought to be ruling it by now."

"That is not my desire." He didn't want to rule; he wanted to live without doing too much damage. He wanted God to forgive what he had become.

By the sneer in his lips and his half-lidded gaze, Eduardo did not seem to think much of Ricardo.

"You must come to see the Mistress in Mexico City."

"Why?" Ricardo said.

"Because it will be better if you come to her rather than making her send someone for you."

Again, Ricardo resisted the urge to draw his sword. After all, he had questions, too. "All right. I will come to the city to visit your Mistress. How will I find her?"

"The same way we found each other tonight. You have so very much to learn, Don Ricardo."

Yes, that was what he was afraid of.

Henri got up to meet him when Ricardo rode into the estancia some hours before dawn. Holding aloft a lantern, he waited at the front of the courtyard and shouted a greeting. Ricardo waved in reply. Henri was a short, dark-skinned man with unruly black hair and crow's-feet at his eyes that gave him a perpetual smiling look. Ricardo had known him since he'd been born, had known his parents since *they* were born. The continuity of it was strange and wonderful. This was the closest Ricardo would ever have to a family of his own, and he valued it.

"Feliz Navidad, sir," Henri said, taking the animal's reins as Ricardo dismounted. "How was your trip?"

"Eventful," Ricardo said. A rock still sat at the pit of his stomach. The world had not shifted yet—but it was about to.

"Oh?"

Ricardo didn't elaborate. They worked together to untack and feed his horse, rub him down and put him away. Even the animals here had to adjust to a nocturnal schedule, poor things.

When he first arrived here, this place had been a failed mission overseen by the demonic Fray Juan and his bloodthirsty caballeros. They had tried to recruit Ricardo. Failed. He'd stayed and tried to turn the old church and outbuildings into something resembling a working estancia. In exchange for destroying the demons who'd hunted them, a local village helped him. They worked the land, herded sheep—and gave him a public face to protect his nighttime secret. He built onto the church and transformed it into a rather elegant home. Nothing so grand as a palace, but it had a courtyard and garden, a patio, a well, and several fine rooms. He'd filed all appropriate documents with the government—on paper, he was the owner and landlord here. Already he'd twice posed as his own son to ensure he maintained ownership of his lands. It didn't take much—an embarrassed bow of his head, a careful explanation that yes, he was an unfortunate by-blow, but for lack of other heirs his father had acknowledged him as his own, and here was the paper and will to prove it.

Eternal life required so much planning, those of his countrymen who had searched for the Fountain of Youth had no idea.

Ricardo washed up while Henri stoked the fire in the sitting room's hearth. Dawn was coming soon—the sky outside was turning gray, and he felt the weight of approaching sunlight in his bones.

"What happened?" Henri asked.

"I met another one. A man like me."

Henri stilled for a moment, then hung the poker on its hook and came to sit across from Ricardo at the table. "I thought you were the only one, apart from the ones who made you like this."

"So did I. I . . . it seems this is all much more complicated."

"What does it mean?" Henri asked.

"I do not know. But I must go to the city to find out."

"It is too dangerous—"

"If I don't, they will come here."

"There . . . there is more than one other?"

"So I gather." He tapped a hand on his leg and stared at the low flames writhing in the hearth. The warmth on his face felt good, but he had to sleep soon—in the cellar, underground, without windows and danger of sunlight.

"Have you eaten tonight, sir?"

"No, I haven't." He hadn't thought of it, not even when

Eduardo assaulted Marie. What he was attributing to anxiety might simply be hunger.

Without further prompting, Henri fetched a cup from the sideboard and drew a knife from the sheath at his belt. He made a quick, shallow cut across his forearm, and blood welled. His movements were practiced, and in a minute or two he'd dripped a good amount of the stuff into the cup. Both his arms had lines and scars from many similar cuts. The arms of many of the people who lived here did. Ricardo was milking these people like cows.

"Thank you," he said, taking the cup from Henri. He always said thank you, every time.

He thought he could remember the way wine or brandy felt, drinking a whole cupful after coming in out of the cold. The way it hit the belly like fire and flowed through his limbs. The blood felt like that, tasting of comfort, lighting his nerves from within. He closed his eyes, sighed out a breath of pleasure, and yes, he felt better. Perhaps the problem of Eduardo was not so difficult. Perhaps this would all come to nothing.

"Thank you," he said again. He could never thank Henri and the others enough.

"It is all for the good," Henri said, and he sounded honest and true. This wasn't a nicety; he meant it. "We keep you safe because you keep us safe. We are family. A strange family, but still a family."

Ricardo stood and clasped the man's shoulder before retreating to his underground chamber.

The journey to Mexico City was some four hundred miles. It would take two weeks at good speed. He and Henri acquired a wagon and horses to pull it, provisions, and imaginary trade business to explain himself. The wagon had no windows. During daylight hours, Ricardo slept in a crate to protect him from sunlight. In this manner, with Henri driving the wagon, they were able to travel by day, which made the journey faster. At night, Ricardo awoke and managed their affairs. They were usually able to find inns and carry on as any other travelers would. A couple of nights, they needed to sleep on the road, but both men had managed without roofs before.

One of Henri's sons, sixteen-year-old Suerte, came along, both to learn the business of making such a journey and also to bleed for Ricardo. Henri couldn't sustain him alone for the whole journey, so the two took turns.

His father slept early, but Suerte stayed up some nights to keep Ricardo company while he stood watch. And to ask for stories. Suerte's appetite for stories was vast.

"Tell me again about Coronado," Suerte asked, sitting by the fire with his back to a piñon, carving on a walking stick.

"I've told you everything I remember about Coronado."

"You say that every time, and every time you remember something new. So I keep asking. What was he like after the expedition? You don't talk very much about that."

"Because it's very sad. He was a broken man. He was supposed to find not only his own fortune but everyone else's. He was supposed to bring glory to Spain. He did none of these. I remember him slumped as he rode, his dented helm tied to his saddle. He couldn't even look up, as if he depended on his horse to know the way home."

"Did you love him?"

"I hardly even spoke to the man. There were hundreds of us in his company, after all. I'm not sure he even knew my name. But I followed him because I believed in him. I believed in the stories, and I believed that Spain would spread all over this continent to make a great empire. I . . . don't believe any of that now."

"How big is this continent?"

"It's taking us weeks to simply travel between Zacatecas and the capital. Imagine this journey multiplied a hundred times over, then double it. That is how much land there is north of us. In Coronado's company we never came close to the end of it."

Suerte sighed in amazement, the wonder of it filling his vision. Ricardo grinned wryly. "You would break your father's heart if you decided to trek north to find your fortune and leave the running of the estancia to him and Tomas."

"They would be happy to have me out of their hair."

"Maybe for a week, but no more."

The boy gouged a particularly rough cut from his carving. He was restless; the estancia was confining, and he wanted an adventure. To be his own man, not his father's son and Tomas's brother. Ricardo had to remember how he was as a boy—he'd been only a couple of years older than Suerte when he left Spain to make his fortune in the colony. He had no way of explaining that once a boy left on such an adventure, he would age quickly, live more life than the actual years, and he could never go back. Boys never understood, did they?

"Are you laughing at me?" Suerte asked.

"No," Ricardo said. "I'm smiling at the patterns. Life is patterns. It's comforting, somehow."

The boy furrowed his brow, confused, and went back to his carving without a word.

Ricardo left Henri and Suerte at the edge of the city, unwilling to bring them to the attention of Eduardo and his friends. His first nightfall in the city, he dressed in his finest suit, pulled a gold-trimmed velvet cloak over his shoulder, put on his sword, and set out.

He had been back to the city once or twice in the last century, and each time it seemed utterly transformed. He felt he would have to remove entire layers of it to see anything that he recognized. It wasn't just that Spanish civilization had become fully entrenched here. No, more that the entire world was changing, and quickly. Buildings growing taller than ever, churches becoming more ornate than he could have imagined. The streets themselves were better: more skillfully paved, more comfortable. He was traveling through time, into the future, one day at a time, forever.

On a hunch he went to the wealthiest neighborhood, where the governor and commissioners had their palaces and the wealthiest merchants and landlords aspired to live. Here, the streets were wide, and the houses and courtyards sat behind walls with filigreed iron gates. Some folk had found their fortunes in the New World, obviously.

He wandered the streets of this neighborhood, imagining himself a shadow. A few guards and carriages passed by; they did not notice him. But in less than an hour he felt that ice in the middle of his spine, the chill of another unholy presence approaching. He stopped and turned, taking stock, making sure he could watch all avenues of approach.

And there was Don Eduardo, standing in the middle of the street as if he had appeared from nothing. Ricardo approached, imagining himself some acquaintance who had simply met him on the road, under a normal sun.

Eduardo's smile seemed pleased. "You came! I very much hoped you would."

"How could I refuse your invitation?" Let the man interpret whatever bite he would from Ricardo's tone.

The prickling sense at the back of his neck continued, and more shadows took on life, figures emerging, visible now only because they wished to be. A gentleman in brown with riding boots; another in a short cape. A woman in her thirties wearing a gown of dark velvet. Her pale hair was braided into a crown around her head. Ricardo glanced at each of them in turn, acknowledging that he was surrounded. The situation recalled a memory of a long-ago confrontation, when Fray Juan's four knights of darkness surrounded him, attacked him, made him one of them.

But that was a long time ago, and Ricardo was not so easily injured these days. He waited to see what they would do.

"Eduardo! You didn't tell us how beautiful he is!"

Ricardo had just enough blood in his veins to blush at this.

"Didn't I? Ah well, I apologize for the omission," the man answered.

"The Mistress must see him," the man in the short cape said. His beard was neat, and he had a hard look about his eyes. Ricardo had no way of telling how old any of them were. They all looked of an age, but they might have lived a thousand years.

The woman with golden hair stepped toward him, her wide skirt shushing as she moved, elegant as any court lady. She put a seductive sway in her step, gazing demurely down her fine nose. "Now he is wondering who we all are, where we all came from."

"I suspect you are come from Spain."

She studied him, revealing the sharp points of her teeth in an amused smile.

"Please do come with us, señor. I should so very like to know you better." The woman moved to hook her arm through his.

"Forgive me, my lady, for I have not yet formally introduced myself. I am Don Ricardo de Avila, and I am pleased to meet you." He stepped back and made a very proper bow, as if they danced in some fine hall in Spain.

The woman's eyes shone. She appeared delighted. "Ooh, you are very fine *indeed*. I am the Lady Elinor." She curtsied just as precisely, then took up Ricardo's arm and tucked her own in the crook of his elbow. In his old life such familiarity would have astonished him, and he would have stammered as he tried to hide any sign of attraction to her. Now, though, they were merely two hunters in the same territory. Perhaps allies, perhaps rivals, who could say which? He was wary.

He placed his hand over hers, securing her to his side. Her skin was as cold as his own. Together with Eduardo, they made a small procession to an alleyway that led to a villa, one of the more modest in the neighborhood. The liveried footman who opened the gate for them was human. He seemed quite ordinary, middle-aged, his gaze downcast, deferential. His skin was tan, his hair dark; he might have been mestizo. Ricardo wondered, did he know that he served demons? Did he know who dwelled here?

They continued across a courtyard and to a set of double doors made of some rich carved wood. Another human footman opened these doors.

Inside the villa, the chill and power of the demons loomed large. Some terrible mystery waited for him here, another revelation that the world was not as it seemed, and everything was about to change. Could he survive this new change as he had survived his first transformation?

He hesitated, pulling against Elinor's arm. "Are you afraid?" she said, hiding a laugh.

Considering a moment, he found that he wasn't. "This feels rather like making one's first confession as a boy. One hardly knows what to expect."

They all stared at him, and he wondered what about the statement shocked them. Then he realized: he had probably been inside a church more recently than any of them. This thought made him smile, which no doubt only confused them more.

Guided by Elinor, he strode on and imagined himself walking into his own parlor.

He had not been in a room like this since he left Madrid. A true palace, with marble floors and painted ceilings, gilt accents on furniture, tapestries on the walls. The smell of beeswax candles saturated the walls. Shadows lingered on every surface.

More devils came out to meet him. Twelve of them, men

and women in their primes. He could not tell how old they really were, how long they had walked this earth, beautiful and elegant, dressed in the height of fashion. If Ricardo were more vain, he would have been chagrined at his own clothing, which he realized now was a decade or more out of style. He had not been paying attention as he should. No matter. If he cared for fashion, he would live here in the capital, not on his remote estancia. Or he would go back to Spain.

Eduardo and his entourage joined the others, so the whole court of them spread out around him. Elinor let him go and went to her place among them, leaving him alone in the center of the floor, as if he were the focus of some tribunal.

Proud, pleased, wicked, all of it, Eduardo stepped forward. Ricardo recognized the look—his old acquaintance Diego, the man who had brought him to Fray Juan, had looked like that.

"Welcome, Don Ricardo! It gives me great pleasure to introduce you to our patroness. Our Mistress. The reason for our being here."

All the devils in the guise of lords and ladies turned to the back of the room, where a great velvet armchair stood on a shallow dais. A woman in black silk and cloth-of-gold reclined there as if bored, gazing with heavy-lidded eyes. She looked young but seemed ancient, centuries pressing out of her like waves of cold from a block of ice. Her skin was olive, her features not particularly fine, but they had strength in the set of her jaw and brow. Her dark hair lay loose around her shoulders, a few clips set with gemstones pinned on locks here and there. She gave the impression of being a woman of great power who had the luxury of not caring too terribly much what happened around her because her fortress would always remain secure.

The men and women of this court waited to see what he would do when confronted with this startling vision of a woman on an almost-throne. Their gazes were heavy on him.

Eduardo addressed the woman. "Mistress Catalina, I bring to you Don Ricardo de Avila y Zacatecas, of whom I spoke—our mysterious hidalgo de la noche. Don Ricardo, you are in the presence of La Reina Catalina."

She was not the queen. As subjects of the Spanish crown—technically speaking, he supposed—they had only one queen. Yet all of them bowed to her as if she were a queen. No—they would not abase themselves so deeply for His Majesty King Philip. This was more than a noble lady with her attendants. There was power here, ropes of it between Catalina and the others. They were linked; he could feel it.

She had turned them all as Fray Juan had turned him. Turned them, made them hers, and they seemed grateful for it. Unlike him.

Ricardo offered only the respectful bow he would to any noblewoman in her home. "Doña."

Remaining silent, she held the tableau for some time. Finally, in a calm voice that matched her demeanor, she said, "Don Ricardo. The gentleman who should not exist. Eduardo has told you this, hasn't he?"

"Yes, he has, señora. And yet I am here. I confess—I do not understand."

Catalina leaned forward, and her acolytes watched as if witnessing a duel. "Do you know what you are, sir?"

He swallowed, and his breath caught—he did not have to breathe since that night he had died and been reborn as the monster. If he wanted to speak, he had to concentrate to draw breath, and for just a moment he'd forgotten. He had never spoken the words aloud. He had never explained it. Not to a stranger.

"I am a demon," he said.

The woman laughed. "Who told you that?"

Ricardo was used to standing straight, schooling his features so no emotion showed—he had to, in order not to rip apart everyone around him in bloodlust. This was only one of the things he had learned. So he remained calm.

"A man named Fray Juan. The one who made me."

Now the woman frowned, and the expression revealed what she might be like when she was angry, when she sought vengeance. "I do not know this man. Where is he now?"

"I—destroyed him, señora. I drove a spear through his heart."

"You destroyed your Master."

"He made me, but he was not my Master."

No one was breathing. No one here needed to, but they did not even have breath to gasp. Catalina murmured, "Extraordinary."

"Señora, I beg your pardon but I must ask—what am I? What are we?"

"My dear Don Ricardo, you are a vampire."

Knowing the word did not change anything. But there was a word for it. Vampire. A foreign word—not Latin, not even Greek. Something even older then, and stranger. Well then. He nodded thoughtfully and kept on as before.

"You destroyed your Master—the one who made you,"

Catalina repeated. "Did you take his place? Did you take his blood?"

Ricardo didn't understand the question. "He turned to ash before my eyes when I impaled him."

"So his blood—his power—was wasted?"

He was thinking quickly now, taking what little he knew and interpreting this new information. Was she saying that a vampire could take blood from another vampire and thereby take some of his power? Vampires reproduced by draining a victim, then feeding the victim from the vampire's own veins to replace the blood. But did this mean vampires could feed on each other? Take power from one another in this manner? Fray Juan had been very old—very powerful. Then again, perhaps not so powerful.

"Even if I had known I could have done such a thing, I still wouldn't have taken his power. He—was not a good man."

Some of the entourage murmured to one another as if he had said something shocking. Catalina continued studying him. Ricardo knew better than to meet her gaze.

"Even though I never met the man, I am inclined to agree with you. He came to this country without permission. The Master of all Spain sent *me* to establish the first vampire Family in the colony. You can understand then why we are all so interested to find you already here."

Ricardo wasn't thinking so much about that as he was: there was a Master vampire of all Spain? Had there always been one? Did every nation have vampires? How many were there, and how had they kept themselves secret? Well, this last question he could answer—he'd done it himself.

He chuckled. It all seemed so strange. "My lady, I feel

something like a child who has been lost in the forest and raised by wild animals. I know nothing of any of this. I cannot explain it to you. Fray Juan came here, obviously. He made four other . . . vampires . . . before he made me. He wanted to rule this land. To bleed it dry, you might say. He was mad."

"So you killed him," Catalina said. "And the other four as well?"

Again, he bowed, affirming this. And now he had just admitted to killing five vampires before a room full of vampires. Perhaps he ought to think of a plan of escape.

"As I said, they were all quite mad. I did not agree to their plan, and I had to defend myself. I have been alone ever since. For a hundred years now—"

The Mistress raised her hand to stop him. "Never say your age. Among our kind age is strength and power. To tell your age is to tell others exactly what your strengths and weaknesses are. We do not say our ages."

He knew so little, and he did not trust that anything Fray Juan had taught him was true. Catalina must have thought the same thing, because she continued the lesson. "We live in Families for survival, to protect each other, to ensure our safety against those who would destroy us. You must know that the world is full of those who would destroy us. How is it that you have survived all this time alone?"

"I do not know," he said. "As best I could, I imagine." He had made friends from the first, and they had protected each other.

"Eduardo, call for some refreshment," she said to the gentleman. He bowed and left through a door in the back of the room.

Liveried servants—so many servants in this place—returned moments later with platters holding colored glass goblets, enough for everyone. Ricardo smelled the blood in them.

When the tray was offered to him, he took a cup and nodded thanks. He did not ask where it had come from, whom they had taken this from and how, and if those people—this much blood would have had to come from more than one—were still alive or if they had been killed. It wasn't just that he might not like the answer; he had the feeling it would be impolite to ask at all. At least they had not laid a child in front of him and expected him to kill it, as Fray Juan had done all those years ago.

The other devils—vampires—in the room waited for their Mistress. When she had her glass, she raised it high in a toast. "To Don Ricardo, welcome. We are so very glad to meet you and bring you into our fold." She drank, and all her fellows raised their glasses and drank, too.

Ricardo hesitated for a moment, considering her words. He wasn't sure he liked them. But he drank. The blood was still warm, and it filled him like fire.

Whoever's blood this was tasted as if he had been afraid.

He watched the others over the rim of the cup to see how they drank, how they managed—was this a perfunctory matter of survival? No—they indulged. Their throats worked, swallowing the sustenance. They made small moans and sighed with pleasure. Elinor's expression of bliss—eyes half-lidded, lips parted, chin tipped up—was nearly erotic.

From her throne, Catalina watched him. He was sure he was being judged. How was the feral child behaving? Was he truly one of them? Ricardo sipped the blood as he would a decent brandy after dinner. Ran his tongue along his teeth to get every drop of it. Enjoyed, in spite of himself, the warm rush of power the drink provided. Made no other overt display.

"You have probably never had any instruction in the laws of hospitality among our kind," Catalina said, seeming to revel in her role as instructor. She seemed practiced at it. "When you bring a vampire into your space, you are obligated to provide sustenance. Failing to do so invites a wild chaos. To be a Master means you provide for all your people." She gestured to the glittering beauty of her entourage. "This is the true display of power. Do you understand?"

The vampire Family was a like royal court. She provided for them; they served her. He understood very well, and he wanted to go home now.

She set her cup on a table, rose from her throne, and approached. Her court moved aside, fawning. Ricardo stood his ground as she touched his sleeve, studied his face, and finally took his hand as a mother might a child's. Her gaze traced his features; he would not let her look into his eyes. Which was awkward, when she stood this close.

She said, "Ricardo. I am very sorry your time thus far has been spent alone and unsupported. I cannot imagine. You have my deepest sympathies."

"Thank you, my lady."

"But no longer. This is my territory now, and you are no longer alone. We will take care of you." Her smile was gracious, serene. She expected him to be glad of this pronouncement.

But what if he didn't want them to take care of him? He

only wanted to go back to Zacatecas and live—exist, rather—as he always had. But he did not feel he was being given a choice.

He replied as carefully and firmly as he could. "I am very grateful to you for your hospitality. But I have a home, you see. I would like to return there, to continue living as I have. Perhaps I could visit you from time to time."

Eduardo's hand tightened on the pommel of his rapier. That small gesture told Ricardo much.

Catalina was polite, calm, careful. She was too controlled, too powerful, to reveal any slip of emotion. "I am not sure you understand the situation. I cannot let you do that. Your home is my home now. It is how things are done."

"Is it?" Ricardo said coolly.

She gave a flirting smile. "I can't have you plotting behind my back now, can I?"

"I wouldn't do that," he said. While it was a statement of fact, no one here would believe him. Because they would all plot behind Catalina's back, if they had his resources.

She nodded, seeming to concede the point. "As you yourself have stated, there is so much you don't yet understand. I would count it a personal favor if you would stay with us for at least a few days, to help you know us better. Then perhaps I will understand *you* better."

Such a reasonable invitation, but her tone still suggested: prisoner. Ricardo bowed, acceding to the request.

"Dawn comes soon. Eduardo, show our guest to a room. Show him how we care for our favored people."

"My lady," Eduardo answered. In fact, he came to Ricardo's shoulder in the manner of a guard to a prisoner.

"Gracias," Ricardo said. "And Happy Christmas to you, Doña Catalina."

He was rather pleased at the chilled, shocked looks that brought on.

Catalina stared. "You are very strange, señor."

He merely bowed. The scent of blood lingered amidst the smoke of candles.

The room was comfortable. No—it was opulent. Finer than any room in his family's manor back in Spain. Silk and velvet, a wide bed and gilt fixtures. Ricardo had grown used to the merely practical.

The windows were all boarded shut. How sad, that he only felt safe in rooms where the windows were boarded shut. And yet, always, he knew when the sun rose, when daylight was near. The weight of it turned his bones to ice. So he took off his boots, removed his cloak and doublet, and stretched out on the too-soft bed to sleep out the day.

He awoke instantly.

For a time he lay in bed, sure that someone had knocked on the door, or perhaps merely waited outside, listening. Of course, Catalina would set spies on him.

He could not stay here. Not even for the few days the Mistress had suggested. He had refused to be one of Fray Juan's minions, he would not be one of hers. Wasn't Mexico large enough for both of them to have space to keep to themselves?

Space was not the issue, he supposed.

Quickly, he dressed, then stood at the door, waiting for that feeling of ice along his spine. Here in Catalina's den, vampires were everywhere, and that sense was dull and constant—but it wasn't urgent, and it wasn't right outside. He tried the handle, was not surprised to find the door locked.

He squeezed, wrenched, and broke the handle off. The sound of ripping wood was satisfying, but loud—he'd have to move quickly. Fortunately, the next room was dark. He imagined himself a shadow and, keeping his sword still by his leg, he moved as quickly and quietly as he could. Running any of these demons through with his sword would not kill them. He wondered if he should even carry it, but it was an old habit, and the weapon's weight steadied him.

He had other weapons, other tools. Ideally, he would not kill any of them. He suspected that if he destroyed one, he would have to destroy them all. He had been through that once before. While Catalina appeared refined and lovely seated on her throne, a power held her aloft and filled the room. Fray Juan could not have stood against her.

Fray Juan had not told him very much, in the end. But he had learned much on his own. To escape, Ricardo must be like a shadow and slip out of here. Vanish before the light of day rose.

He passed through successive rooms—and got lost. The house was very large indeed, and one room ran into another. At every doorway he paused—vampires did not have heartbeats, so he watched for other cues, for the growing chill on his spine, the urgent tingle at the back of his neck that told him they were near. The trouble was, this building was filled with them. Every doorway held danger. Each room might be the one where Eduardo was waiting for him.

Instead, he paused and listened for a current of air. He did not search for danger but for a way out. In this way he discovered the scent of smoke from evening cook fires, and of the often-rank air of a city with too many horses, dogs, rats, and people crammed into too small a space.

He could follow that thread out of here, like Theseus in the labyrinth.

"Señor, you must stop."

The vampire who found him wasn't Eduardo or Catalina. This was a man whose thinness made him look particularly young. His doublet hung on him a size too large, as if he was trying to make himself bigger. He wore a rapier, but like Ricardo's, it seemed mostly a prop on which to put his hand. Pietro. The boy's name was Pietro, and Ricardo saw when he turned that he must have only been seventeen or eighteen. How maddening, to go through eternity with looks that invited everyone to treat you as a child. He might be a thousand years old, for all Ricardo knew. But no—this one didn't feel old. He had not yet learned to use his youth as a weapon, inviting folk to underestimate him. He wasn't yet so powerful.

"Señor," Ricardo said with a respectful bow. "I was not sure anyone was awake yet."

"The others are about. I'm sure the Mistress would like to speak with you."

The boy was not experienced enough to be wary of Ricardo. He thought he was safe in the fortress of his mistress. Pietro met Ricardo's gaze straight on.

Ricardo spoke gently, stepping toward the boy, holding his gaze, trapping him. "Pietro. I am just a poor country gentleman. This place, your Mistress—I fear it is all too rich for me. Far too complicated to understand. I am overcome, and so I flee back to my simple life. You can explain this to your Mistress, that I am poor and simple, and it would be best for you all to leave me alone and in obscurity. You will never hear from me again."

The boy stared, lips parted, gaze vacant. He nodded, just a little. "We will never hear from you again," he murmured.

"That's right. Really, it's for the best that you let me go."

"Yes. It's for the best."

"Indeed. Muchas gracias to you, señor." He bowed again, and the boy nodded, the tension of confusion around his lips.

Ricardo left the boy staring at a wall as if it held the answer to some great problem. Moving quickly, he followed the currents in the air to a servants' door in back of the house—it wasn't barred, it wasn't guarded. Two human women were there, collecting the day's washing, that was all. They were even easier to deceive than Pietro had been. "I heard a noise in the hallway, you should go see what it is." They blinked, startled, and fled to do exactly what he suggested.

Just like that, he was outside under a wide open sky, hazy with the glow from evening torches and fires. He would not be happy until he was north again and could see the great wash of stars in the black sky of true night. He fled, using his skill and power to move swiftly, like mist. He hadn't fed tonight; he grew more tired than he liked. He had little choice, though.

In short order he found the inn where Henri and Suerte were waiting for him. By scent, by the feel of their particular souls in the air, he found their room.

They jumped, startled, when he swung open the door—they hadn't heard him, and he had forgotten to knock.

"Ricardo!" Henri exclaimed. "What happened to you?"

"I'll tell you on the road. We must be away. We have preparations to make."

Both man and son looked frightened, so they had some idea of what they might be facing. "But what—"

"I will explain. Let's go."

His estancia was not very defensible. A memory intruded from when Coronado's company lay siege to a Zuni city, in the far north. City—little more than a group of clay houses clustered together. But it was on a mesa, surrounded by open plain, and for all their primitive weapons those people had defended themselves well. Ricardo remembered.

He wished for high ground now rather than this pleasant valley. He did not know what sort of assault Catalina and her people could manage, if they would come themselves in the dark of night, mounting a vampire battle of shadows and blood, or if she had a company of human soldiers, mercenaries perhaps, who would come in daylight to attack his people while Ricardo slept and could do nothing about it.

He did not know how much time he had to prepare, how much time Catalina would need to find this place. He, Henri, and Suerte had rushed home as quickly as a wagon and horse could manage, which wasn't quickly at all.

He wished he could believe that Catalina would leave him alone, but it was clear, even in the short time he'd spoken with her, that she saw him as a rival. That all vampires would see him as a rival. That battle he'd fought a hundred years ago against Fray Juan and his men—he would have to fight it all over again.

Over, and over, and over again, every time he encountered one of them. He just wanted to be left alone.

He set his people to building a palisade and wondered if he ought to call in a priest to consecrate one of the buildings here. Make it a church where vampires could not enter.

But that would not stop human soldiers.

They worked by torchlight to sharpen logs while others of his people dug trenches in which to mount them, an angry fence to keep out invaders. Also, they had plenty of bows and arrows—the women made more, as many as they could, and he instructed the archers to aim for the heart. Wooden stakes were death to vampires; he hoped wooden arrows were the same.

Catalina would say he was mad to instruct and arm his people who might now rise up against him. But Ricardo trusted them. It was why he would not hand them over to her rule.

Ricardo paused to look over the defenses taking shape. "We are being invaded," he observed, because yes, he was transforming his beautiful estancia into a fortress.

"Again," Henri said with a huff.

Ricardo had to think about that a moment. He smiled, but he wasn't pleased.

He had been in battle. Ostensibly, his education had prepared him to fight, to lead armies, to conquer. He imagined every scenario that might come to pass if Catalina sent Eduardo and an army of vampires and their enspelled human servants against the estancia. He couldn't imagine it, because he didn't know the size of this army. He didn't know if they would bring weapons. He didn't know anything about *who they were.*

He had fought vampires before—four of them, plus the Master, Fray Juan. He had done it by ambushing, by building traps. By believing he had nothing to lose, that he was already dead. That he had destroyed them, that he had *won,* still came as a shock to him sometimes.

This coming battle was different, because now he had territory to defend. *People* to defend, the grandchildren and great-grandchildren of those who had been terrorized by Fray Juan. Those he had worked with to build this small, comfortable shelter. Henri, the others—they didn't understand what was coming for them.

How did Ricardo prepare them? How did you build a defense against a force you knew so little about? How did you use what skills and weapons you had to defeat such a force? Well, he would have to do what he'd done before: tricks. Ambush.

What would Catalina not expect? What would truly stop her for all time?

Certainly not a battle.

"Don Ricardo, what is wrong?" Henri was concerned.

Ricardo had been staring absently, his mind elsewhere, for a long time. He had thought of something. Not a consecrated church, but . . . something.

"Keep building the wall," he told Henri. "I must see to something."

It was the next night when Catalina's army came to the estancia's palisade. A dozen men on horseback, all vampires, and another dozen on foot carrying wooden spears. Vampire-killing spears. On second glance, he noticed two of the riders were women, but in leather riding clothes, carrying rapiers like the men. They were old. Who could say where they had learned to fight? Ricardo didn't doubt they could.

Half of the army held torches as well as weapons, and a sphere of orange light engulfed them. The scent of smoke was dense. They would burn down his home.

Catalina was not among them, and this told him something about the Masters and Mistresses among the vampires. They remained safe behind their walls, behind their followers. They relied on their followers, without whom they had little power. A useful bit of knowledge there.

Ricardo stood alone at the open gate and faced them. He had sent everyone else inside the house for safety.

"Don Ricardo!" One of the riders urged his mount, a handsome black beast, a few steps forward. It was Eduardo, whose voice was amiable enough, but whose frown was stern. "The most gracious Reina Catalina is saddened that you rejected her hospitality. She hopes you will reconsider and return with us to the city."

"It is a strange hospitality that you must force it upon me."

"Is this your home? Your estancia?" He gestured expansively, to take in the fence and all that lay behind it. "No wonder you feel that you don't need our lady's patronage."

"It is not my estancia," Ricardo said, his smile easy but his stance ready. He'd hidden a bundle of spears within arm's reach, leaning up behind the first section of fence. He waited to see how this played out.

Eduardo pursed his lips. "Oh?"

"Indeed," Ricardo said, watching his toe scuff innocently at a tuft of grass.

"Her ladyship has sent me to bring you back within her fold, as is right and just for one of our kind."

"I will not go," he said.

"Then I—we—will take you. We will take all of this and destroy it. Destroy all you have so that you'll have no choice."

"You are welcome to try. But I will defend this place for its master." He took three steps back so that he was behind the wall, across the threshold that marked the boundary of the estancia. He also picked up one of the spears, just in case this did not work. For now, he merely stood with the spear's butt planted on the ground.

"I thought you were wise," Eduardo said, and his mock-friendliness seemed like a shield. "You could be strong, we've all felt it. We would welcome you into our fold. But now I see you wish for your true death. Is that it?"

"I dislike being told what to do."

The way Eduardo's expression hardened, the way he set his spear against the crook of his arm and kicked his horse to a run, put Ricardo in mind of a jousting knight. Eduardo looked like someone who had long experience at the sport. For a moment, Ricardo was sad that they could not be friends.

The horse rocked back on hind feet, sprang into a ground-eating gallop, charging straight for the opening in the wall, directly at Ricardo.

At the last moment, just as the horse's nose touched the threshold, Eduardo reined back hard, shock drawing his features back in terror. Protesting, the horse threw its head straight up, straining against the bit. Its weight fell back, the animal kicked, and Eduardo fell off. Rolled straight off the horse's back and slammed to the ground as the horse shook itself and raced on. Ricardo stepped out of its way. He would have to fetch the animal and bring it back; he was no horse thief.

Eduardo lurched to his feet, unhurt but furious, gripping his wooden spear in both hands as if preparing to drive it through a boar. But he stopped outside the wall, trapped against the threshold.

Ricardo smiled thinly. "I told you, this place is not mine, and you will need an invitation to enter."

"Then how are you—"

"I have an invitation," Ricardo said.

Eduardo threw his spear. It sailed through, and Ricardo deflected it with his own.

The horses were restless, their riders' anxiety spreading. The vampires' human mercenary force seemed young but ready, and Ricardo thought back a hundred years ago to all those naive young men Coronado had brought north with him. Did these men know whom they served?

Eduardo shouted, losing his composure, his warrior's calm. He wasn't used to losing, Ricardo thought. "I have another army to send against you!"

"I am ready for them," Ricardo said, hefting his own spear, swinging it in an arc. He tensed, ready to run, faster than a shadow, unseen and deadly to these poor men.

Catalina's lieutenant raised his hand, the squad of riders

parted, and the human soldiers marched, spears and swords at the ready. Across the wide space, in the flickering torchlight, Ricardo tried to catch each of their gazes. To impart to them the assurance that death awaited if they moved any closer.

"Do not look at him!" Eduardo commanded. "He is but one man! He is only one—"

With a slap and a hiss, a crossbow bolt shot through the air and struck Eduardo through the heart. Ricardo remained calm, but it was an effort. This wasn't part of the plan. He'd told Henri and the others to stay out of it. But there behind the palisade, hidden in the shadows, Suerte crouched holding a crossbow. The vampires had been so focused on Ricardo that they hadn't noticed the heartbeat, the boy's scent of living blood. Or they had discounted him as weak prey.

Suerte remained hidden, and Ricardo didn't look at him, to avoid drawing attention. He gazed out calmly, as if he had willed the crossbow bolt to appear and strike Eduardo dead. And he was now, absolutely, dead. He clutched at the bolt protruding from his chest, sputtered as if he really did have breath and blood to spit from his mouth. Before he could fall, he turned to dust, limbs and extremities going gray, his whole body crumbling into desiccated flesh. The surprised glare in his eyes seemed to be the last part of him to fade.

Ricardo met the gazes of every man who stood before the gate with a weapon in his hand, and he whispered to them, *Go, you cannot win here.*

The soldiers all dropped their spears and fled. The mounted vampires seemed ready to follow them, but Ricardo called out to one of them, whom he recognized from his brief stay in the capital. The woman, Elinor, now looking very different from her painted, elegant self.

"My Lady Elinor," he called. "Will you take a message to Doña Catalina for me?"

She hesitated, perhaps wondering if this was some trick. "Yes," she said finally. "You did not have to kill him."

"Apparently I did." He spared a quick smile for Suerte. "Tell Catalina this: this estancia is protected. I would ask that she leave it alone, now and forever. In return, I will leave. She can have Mexico. All of it, as she was promised, as she expected. I will leave this country, and she'll never see me again."

"Where will you go? Back to Spain? To France?"

He imagined a country filled with vampires, with Masters and Mistresses all like Catalina, and himself trying to move among them, keeping to himself, convincing them he was no danger. He shook his head.

"No. I will go north to the borderlands. That is all you need to know, and you will never hear of me again."

Strangely, the woman smiled. "Never is a very long time, Don Ricardo. I think we may hear of each other again someday. You will tell me stories of what you have seen."

He offered her a respectful bow, and for just a moment regretted that he could not spend more time here.

"We will deliver your message."

"Gracias."

She wheeled her horse around, and the others followed. The riders trotted away after the soldiers who'd fled before.

Now he could deal with Suerte. "I would have managed them," he said.

The boy—not so much a boy anymore, he was sixteen and sure of himself—picked himself off the ground. He slung the crossbow easily over his shoulder.

"Of course. But a little help never hurt, eh?"

Together, they returned to the manor.

The house's main sitting room was directly through the front doors, across the courtyard. Comfortable chairs were gathered around a fireplace, tables held vases of flowers, and borders had been painted on the stucco walls over the years by anyone with talent and a desire. Blue and yellow flowers looped around each other in a vine-like pattern near the ceiling, and a geometric pattern in red lines framed the hearth. The room was warm, lived in, and Ricardo spent most of his time here when he wasn't working or sleeping. Originally, this had been the main part of the church Fray Juan was supposedly presiding over. Ricardo had taken it over, knocked down walls, expanded it, made it a home. In the next room, a trapdoor led to his cellar bedroom—windowless, forever dark. That was the only room of Fray Juan's he had kept.

He wondered what Henri would do with that room when he was gone. Turn it into a root cellar perhaps. Or seal it up.

The whole family had gathered. Henri, his wife Madalena, their oldest son Tomas and his wife Juana, Suerte, and several of their other children. A large, contented family who'd built this place into a village. Ricardo was proud of what they'd done here.

He sat in a large cushioned chair, his hand resting on a

bundle of papers on the table. "All that remains is to file the papers with the provincial governor's office in Zacatecas. You are now my heir, and this is all yours."

Henri looked stricken. The others were uncertain, looking to him for how to respond.

"This is only a paper," he said. "A fiction—"

"No, it is not. It is all yours. It's the only way to keep the vampires out, and to keep you all safe, as I promised your grandparents I would. So you will be Don Henri, and I will leave."

As soon as he said the words aloud, his heart lifted. At least, what was left of his heart lifted. Facing this change, this upheaval—he could no longer see into the future, and it felt good. He felt like he had when he had boarded the ship in Spain a century before.

He didn't know if he'd ever be able to convince them this was truly what he wanted to do. Madalena rushed forward, kneeling at his feet, clasping his hands. "Ricardo, no, this is your home! Haven't we always taken care of you? Doesn't our blood run through your veins?"

He squeezed her hands in return. "I will miss you all, truly. But I feel the need to seek out an adventure. Go north and light a candle for my old commander."

"I will go with you," Suerte said, stepping forward.

Both Madalena and Henri started, "No—"

"You'll need someone to look after you." Suerte spoke only to Ricardo; he knew whom he had to convince here.

And, Ricardo realized, he would need someone. Certainly he could attempt to travel and survive on his own. But how much easier his existence would be with someone to seal the doors during the day. Someone to provide a cupful of blood every few days. And Suerte would not need coercing. He felt a gratitude for the young man he'd never be able to express.

He expected the parents to argue further, but Madalena went to embrace her son, proud and sad all at once.

Ricardo looked around at his home and his family that he had fought hard for, that he had enjoyed for decades longer than any man could expect to enjoy home and family. Yes, he would always remember this place fondly. But it was time to go.

In the early years of the border town of Santa Fe, people of all sorts came and went, all the time. Missionaries and traders from the south, the soldiers defending them, native peoples from every direction. Settlers, families, and all the people who followed to carve homes out of the desert land. The place was becoming a crossroads.

In a certain tavern where travelers often stopped before setting out to press even farther west and north, a man could be found with a cup sitting before him that he never drank from. He was obviously of good breeding, with an elegant bearing and an old-fashioned way of speaking. He had a servant, a rough-looking Mexicano of around thirty whom the man treated more as a friend, which was odd, but one could make allowances for the eccentric. The pair acted as translators and guides—they were friendly with many of the Pueblo people and had even successfully negotiated with some Apache. Strangely, though, if you wanted to hire this man for your caravan or as a scout, you had to understand that he only worked at night.

Late at night this man would tell old stories of conquistadors so vividly that he might have been there himself—which was impossible, of course. He was a young man in his prime. When pressed, he said his great-grandfather had been part of Coronado's company, a true conquistador. Much debate went on about whether to believe this.

In the end, he was so comfortable in the border towns, and he gazed over the plains with such appreciation—love, even—everyone felt he must have at least part of the soul of one of those old soldiers.

Dead Men
in Central City

HORSES WERE THE MOST UNRELIABLE, most unfortunate creatures ever to walk the earth. And yet, Ricardo was immensely sad that his was gone. He and his pretty tamed Mustang mare, Bandita, had been back and forth across the West for six years, and now she'd taken a bad step—a hole, a sharp rock, he hadn't been able to figure out which—fallen down a hillside, and broken not one but two legs.

Traveling on horseback through the Rockies at night, accidents happened. His own neck had snapped in the fall, twisting wrong when Bandita came down on top of him. He'd heard the crack. Half an hour of lying still and staring at treetops healed him well enough. But she was mortal. The whole time, he'd listened to Bandita groan in pain, working herself into a sweat as she struggled to stand and fell back again, her broken legs unable to support her. Once he was upright, he'd done the only kind thing he could and ended it for her with his .45. He lay next to her for a time, taking in her last warmth and working to remember her, because she deserved to be remembered. Coiled up a couple strands of hair from her tail because he wasn't sure why. Just that he had a braided band made up of tail hairs from all the horses he'd cared about over the centuries.

He gathered what gear he could carry, saddlebags and blankets, left her to the scavengers and moved on. The sky was turning gray, dawn was close, and he desperately needed a place to bed down for the day. He was in the middle of forest, miles from the next town with no sign of shelter anywhere.

He did not panic. He'd lasted this long and been caught in more unlikely situations than this. He could always find some place out of the sun if he just took a moment and looked. Around here, plenty of mine shafts were dug into the rock, out of the light, if he could find one. The fall had turned him around a bit, but if he remembered right, there were plenty of small towns between here and Denver. Maybe not much more than miners' cabins and a general store, but they'd do.

Finding high ground, he paused and took a deep breath, tasting every scent that came to him. Felt eddies in the air, sensed creatures that had passed this way, and knew what might be waiting for him over the next hill. He found prey, a concentration of warm human blood rising. More than blood, he smelled the smoke of wood and coal fires, masonry and painted wood. The collected smell of horses and livestock kept in corrals. There was a whole town nearby.

Central City. Had to be. If he could get there in time, he might even be able to spend the day in a bed instead of a dank mine shaft. He tasted another breath, checked the direction, murmured a quiet prayer to the gray sky—he still prayed, taking it on faith that He was listening—and *ran*.

Trees blurred; the air turned to wind around him. He drew on some other force, a demonish power that flowed into him from some unknown source. From the first he'd been suspicious of it—but he would use it when he had to. It meant he could *run*. A shadow in the night. If only it were night.

His last bit of borrowed blood turned sluggish in the growing light. He didn't have long. He kept to shaded gulches and gullies—away from the hilltops that would get the first rays of morning sun.

He could smell the town, sense people waking up with the dawn. He might or might not make it. At this moment the only creature more unfortunate than his horse was very likely him.

Then, coming around the next gulch, down the next slope, he found a road. Not much of one—dirt packed down by wagon wheels and dozens of horses. Not a main route, this probably went up to mining claims in the hills. But the way opened up. Just a few more minutes, a few more yards of speed—

And there it was. The mining boomtown of Central City, tucked in the mountains above Denver and looking to Ricardo's eyes like a beacon of civilization. Two main streets intersected each other; another dozen side streets ran off from them. Solid rows of buildings three and four stories tall lined up. Maybe not pretty, not sturdy—the town had grown from nothing in just a few years after all—but it made a good showing.

One storefront had light shining through the windows,

faint with the dawn but still visible. The sign said "SA-LOON" and "ROOMS TO LET." There, he'd go there.

The edges of the peaks sheltering the town lit with golden sun. Ricardo didn't look, he just moved, drawing the very last bit of life in him, very nearly flying down the main street to the saloon door, stumbling inside and slamming it behind him, as the light outside grew.

Inside seemed darker than it should, the lanterns weak and the furniture brown and stained. The mirror behind the bar was dusty. But there were people here, a few who'd stayed up all night drinking and playing cards. They might continue through the day. Three men at a faro table, another at the bar. One behind the bar who might have been the proprietor, and at the back door a matronly looking woman who seemed to be just getting started for the day. For the most part, despite their tired eyes and roughshod appearances, they smelled *good*. Full of warm blood, and he was hungry.

Except—the man behind the faro table smelled ill.

They all glanced up at him and stared. Ricardo imagined he looked a mess. At the best of times he presented a handsome, aristocratic figure, with dark hair, a firm jaw and fine nose. But now he was dusty, grimy, and probably had a panicked gleam in his eyes. He noticed a spatter of blood on his beige shirt from shooting Bandita, and his dark pants were torn. He looked like a man in trouble.

He reminded himself to breathe, so as to appear normal. Straightening, he settled his saddlebags firmly over his shoulder and convinced himself—and the rest of the room, he hoped—that he knew what he was doing.

Stepping up to the bar, he told the man, "I'd like a room.

One without windows if you have it. Or a corner of the cellar if you don't." He set coins on the polished surface of the bar.

The barman stared at him. Swallowed visibly and stammered. "We . . . I mean . . . what do you mean . . . no windows?"

"I mean I'm sensitive to the light. No windows."

"I—I'm sorry. We're all full up."

"You are not all full up, Frank. Sell the man a room, why don't you." The faro dealer spoke with an accent—light, lilting, southern.

The barman really couldn't seem to decide what to do. He glanced back and forth between Ricardo and the dealer like one of them was holding a gun to his head, but he didn't know which. Ricardo didn't have time for this—he couldn't look that terrible, could he? Surely a town like this had seen worse.

Fine. They couldn't do this politely, Ricardo would manage in his own way. He leaned in; Frank gripped the edge of the wood, almost as if he knew what was coming. He watched Ricardo, which made it very easy for Ricardo to catch his gaze. Catch his gaze and fall into it, grabbing hold of a corner of the man's will and *twisting.*

"You'd like to give me a room with no windows. You have something for me, don't you? My money's good here. You're happy to help out." He spoke low, persuasively, and his words filled the man, whose gaze softened. He nodded with understanding.

"We've got . . . something. Not much of a room. More like a closet. But it ain't got windows."

"That'd be fine. I'll take it, and I want to be left alone."

"Right. Sure. Upstairs. Second door on the left."

"And no one will bother me."

"Of course not, sir. Of course." He reached under the counter for a key and slid it across the bar. Ricardo took it gratefully. Only a few more moments and he could collapse. Worry about blood tomorrow.

He turned to the stairs, and out of the corner of his eye saw the faro dealer nod to his players, stand, and nonchalantly make his way over, as if he just happened to want a stroll across the room at that moment, and they just happened to meet at the base of the stairs. The man glanced into the tumbler of whiskey he held, swirling the amber liquid. He also held a handkerchief, which he'd coughed into a couple of times already. Lungs rotting from the inside out—Ricardo could smell it.

Ricardo waited. The man obviously wanted to say something.

"Remind me never to sit down to cards with you, sir," he said finally. His grin seemed amused.

So, the faro dealer noticed that, did he? Ricardo hadn't planned on playing cards; most games of chance weren't, and he wasn't interested. But did this man really understand what he had seen? The hair on the back of Ricardo's neck stood up. "I'm not much for cards myself."

"Your wisdom impresses me."

The gambler stood out with his precise way of speaking, his polite bearing, and his fine clothes. Shirt starched, jacket pressed, tie neatly knotted. He drew the eye, a calm pool in the grungy saloon. A man like him didn't have to go out and dirty himself in the mines and the town, when people would come to him and hand over their money.

"Thank you, Mr.— "

"Doctor, if you please, sir. Doctor John Holliday." The handkerchief disappeared in a pocket, and he held a hand for shaking.

Ricardo knew that name. Everyone knew that name. "A pleasure."

"The pleasure is mine. Gratifying, meeting a fellow man of manners way out here."

"Indeed. My name is Ricardo Avila."

"You are from Mexico?"

"Spain." Really, though, he'd only spent the first seventeen years of his life in Spain, and the next two centuries in Mexico. He sometimes said the latter, when the situation warranted. In this place, he judged it would be better to be from Spain. "Though I have not been back there in some time."

"Won't you have a drink with me, sir? I suspect you have some fine tales to tell of your recent travels." He gestured at his whiskey, nodded to a chair, and Ricardo lamented that it was sunrise. He was dead on his feet, nearly.

"My deep apologies, sir. I need to rest after the night I've had. Can I take up your invitation tonight?"

"Just after sunset, maybe?" Holliday suggested.

And wasn't this ominous? Ricardo had to remember to draw breath in order to answer, "That'll do nicely."

"Tonight then, sir."

Holliday watched him rush up the stairs.

As he'd been informed, the closet had a bed, a chair, barely enough room to navigate around both—and no windows.

Ricardo locked the door, propped the chair in front of it for good measure, and collapsed just as the coming day pulled him out of consciousness. Somehow, he'd made it through another night.

Hours later, the sun set, and he awoke in darkness, uncertain where he was until he retraced his steps. He'd had to kill Bandita. He'd managed to find shelter. And Doc Holliday was dealing faro in the saloon downstairs.

Well then.

His veins burned, his mind throbbed. He didn't get hungry, but his heart gaped, empty. He'd gone several days without new blood. The situation would not stand—he could feel every heart in the place. The saloon had filled with patrons. He didn't just hear their voices echoing against the floorboards. He could hear their hot, beating hearts, and he wanted them all.

He had not lasted this long by not being very careful at times like these.

Even without windows or a lantern, he could see a little. He straightened his clothing, rubbed a hand on his stubbled face. He needed to get cleaned up. He took the chair away and carefully opened the door to look out in the hallway. Fortunately, he only had to wait a moment before the matronly woman from last night appeared, climbing up the stairs.

"Oh sir! You're awake! Been waiting to hear from you—you were quiet as the dead in there."

"No doubt," he said. "If I could trouble you for a few things? A lantern maybe, some water?"

"Sure thing, give me just a minute."

He learned that her name was Hannah O'Shea, she was

the barman's wife, and they made a decent living running this place. When she came to set a basin and lantern on the chair, which was also a washstand apparently, Rick carefully closed the door behind her. She turned at the sound, and he caught her gaze. Murmured words of comfort until she drifted into a stupor, settling on the bed as if she slept. He took her wrist and drank from it.

Not much. Not enough to do serious harm. A few swallows of rich blood, which filled him with fire and life. The burning in his veins settled, the thirst quenched. Hannah might be a little dizzy for the evening, but he held her gaze and reassured her that all was well, she just needed to drink some water and eat a little something, it was probably the heat made her feel a little off. She agreed, apologizing for nodding off like that, and he gently sent her off to the rest of her business.

It was not a perfect system, but it worked well enough in emergencies. He could now safely move among the saloon's patrons without fear of losing himself. Time was, he had friends who knew what he was and were willing to offer up some of their blood for him. He'd been so grateful—not just for the blood but for the companionship. Now—he'd been alone in the wilderness too long.

Denver. Denver would be different.

He washed, shaved, put on his spare shirt—smelled a little of horse, but he aired it out the best he could. Put on his coat. He trusted he made a presentable enough picture.

At last, he emerged. He probably didn't look too awful.

The saloon was exactly what he expected, full of miners and cowboys, workmen and itinerates finishing their day by drinking and gambling the money they'd earned.

The place was popular, the bar and tables full. Several card games were in progress—and yes, Holliday was still at the table against the far wall. A crowd two deep gathered to watch. Man had a reputation, after all.

Ricardo sidled up to lean against the bar, to take stock of the place, to think for a minute about what he needed to do next. Get a horse, get to Denver, settle in. Place like this ought to be just a stop on the road. But he was intrigued. He'd met legends before and known he was seeing something special.

"Get you a drink?" asked the barman—Frank, Ricardo remembered.

"Whiskey," Ricardo said. "Just a bit." He didn't drink—not in the usual sense, anyway—but it was good to have something in hand to blend in. Frank poured him a shot, and Ricardo had a thought. He asked, "How long has Holliday been in town?"

"Just a few days. On his way to Leadville I hear, but there's plenty of action in town, he decided to stay for a few."

"And you get the usual cut?"

He grinned happily, and Ricardo thought about all those miners and prospectors working to get rich at entirely the wrong end of things.

Ricardo leaned in. "You have any work needs doing around here? I'm looking to earn some cash before I head out. And I wouldn't mind sticking around to see the action."

The barman nodded in perfect understanding. He could charge admission to watch Holliday deal faro. "Been a little shorthanded. What all can you do?"

"Anything," Ricardo said.

"Tend bar? Clean the place? Deal with riffraff?"

"Oh yes," Ricardo said, a curl on his lip. He didn't even have to catch the man's gaze and twist his will to make him believe. Holliday brought in business, but he brought in trouble, too, and they were trying to balance the both. A strong young man behind the bar might help with keeping folks in line.

So, Ricardo had a job.

Four nights in, Ricardo had become familiar, part of the furniture. He'd demonstrated his value to Frank—after that first shot of whiskey, he didn't take another drink. Nothing better than a sober barman. He'd stopped two fights already without fuss or trouble. Just grabbed the miscreants by their collars, looked them in the eyes, and walked them out the door. Had a knack for it, Frank observed happily, and gave Ricardo a bonus both times it happened. If regular folk felt safe in his place, they'd come spend their money.

Ricardo could bend this whole town to his will. Gather to himself a whole collection of servants who worshipped him. This was what his kind normally did, what they were made to do.

He'd heard the arguments, and he did not like them. He didn't want servants, he wanted friends, just a few. But they died so quickly, and the older he got, the quicker they died. More than three centuries, and the paradox of his existence was still revealing itself to him.

Holliday was always at his table when Ricardo emerged for the night and rarely retired before he did. Coughing kept him awake, he said, and if he was awake, he might as well be making money. Every couple of hours he'd come to the bar to refill his drink, and he'd talk. Each night, a little more.

"I have heard of some folk having a sensitivity to sunlight," Holliday said, drinking off the last from his tumbler and holding it out for more. Ricardo obliged. "Your condition appears to be most severe."

They had done this dance for four days. Somehow, Holliday knew what he was and seemed to be watching for bodies stashed under the bar, studying Ricardo's mouth for a glimpse of telltale fangs. But Ricardo was very careful.

"I manage," he said. He could always find a man or two in back sleeping it off. A couple of girls he could pay for an hour of company. None of them remembered what he did to them. He never drank from anyone twice. He was able to gather some strength before the next leg of his journey. "As a medical man, you must see that kind of thing a lot."

"Oh, not so much. You have to know what to look for."

"And of course, you do."

The man's mustache shifted as he grinned. "Of course."

"It's a topic you're interested in, I gather."

"Certainly. I've heard such good stories. Like yours. Traveling 'cross the Rockies on horseback at night? Why ever would you do such a thing?"

"The train was all booked up." In fact, the train had been watched, and he couldn't risk getting cornered. After what had happened on this trip, he might risk it next time.

Holliday chuckled. "I can tell you are a man who always finds a way. A survivor."

"Yes," he murmured. "I am that."

"Any advice? For someone who might like to survive?" He waved a hand in a casual gesture, and Ricardo had a strange thought. Holliday was dying, that was clear. Cough by cough, his life ebbed. Ricardo could smell it, a miasma that hung about him—unlike everyone else in the room, he didn't smell like food.

He had no advice. Not really. "I keep to myself. Try not to bother anyone."

"And if they bother you?"

Ricardo glanced at Holliday sidelong. Holliday had never once met his gaze. He looked in his glass, he studied the crowd, traced the grain in the wood of the bar. But he knew better than to look in Ricardo's eyes. Ricardo just about came straight out to ask, *How?* How did he know?

"Well then," Ricardo said. "I send them on their way as politely as I can."

"Amen, sir."

Ricardo had been in Central City for ten days when he figured it was time he moved on. Holliday had made noise about doing likewise. As fascinating as this stop had been, as much as he was sure there were more stories to learn, Ricardo was starting to get a reputation, and people were starting to know him. This was too small a place for that to be healthy for him. He'd been through about as much of his food supply as he could without doubling up and raising questions. Best to get a horse and head on out.

One more night, he decided. One more night of watching Holliday, of watching people watch Holliday, and then maybe he'd have his own story to tell about the man. Holliday had been dealing for an hour or so already. His regulars and more than a few folk passing through surrounded his table and took part in the action. The night was perfectly normal. Which made it all the more jarring when a chair clattered back as a man stood up from the faro table and shouted, "You cheat! You're a lying cheat!"

A young cowboy type stood pointing at Doc Holliday. He was not a regular.

Ricardo set down the cloth he'd been using to wipe down glasses and moved around the bar. The room had gone still, conversation falling quiet, everyone looking over.

A space had formed around the table—a number of players took up their cash and rushed away and couldn't be faulted for it. That left the cowboy type, a beardless kid in boots, trousers, a plain shirt, and bandana around his neck, sandy-colored hair brushing his ears, and a fiery look in his eyes. He wore two six-shooters in holsters on his belt.

Ricardo had a feeling this wasn't about faro.

Holliday hadn't moved. He sat straight as always in his chair, one hand holding his ubiquitous handkerchief, the other tapping on the box from which he'd apparently dealt a double, if Ricardo read the board right. Banker won half the stakes on a double, and Ricardo wondered how many pairs Holliday had dealt out of that box. Didn't really matter, faro was an easy game to cheat at, and in any case you didn't just stand up and call Holliday a cheater. At least, most folks didn't.

"Might you repeat yourself, sir? I don't think everyone heard you clear enough," Holliday said, leaning back.

"You cheat! You fixed the deck!"

The corner of Holliday's lip curled up. "You've been betting so little, how do you even notice you've lost?"

The cowboy looked like he wanted to lunge across the

table at him, but he restrained himself. Ricardo watched, fascinated.

"Doesn't it bother you? Me calling you a cheater?"

"Boy, I've been called so much worse. You seem *quaint* to me."

The young man snarled. But still, he didn't start the fight Ricardo was sure was coming. He was ready to grab whichever fist shot out first.

"Doesn't this blowhard bother any of y'all?" the cowboy called out to the rest of the room, to his fellow players who'd pressed even farther away. "You sit here every night and let him take your money! Why?"

"Kid, you know who that is?" a voice hissed from the crowd, and the cowboy's hard gaze turned straight back to Holliday. Of course he knew exactly who Holliday was. It was why he'd come here, and his expression twisted, trying to come up with something to say that would get the gunfighter out of his chair.

Holliday read him right. He'd probably seen a dozen of these young hotheads in his time. Ricardo hoped Holliday would stay seated, tell the kid to simmer down. Maybe buy him a drink. Not egg him on, because something about this didn't feel right. But alas.

"Your ploy is weak, sir," Holliday said carefully, directing the words like gunfire. "If your intention is to get me out on that street to challenge me on some point of honor—well, my honor's not worth so much. You want to try against me you just need to ask."

"Doctor," Ricardo warned, moving close. The young cowboy had a kind of madness that told him that challenging Doc Holliday was a good idea. He wanted to be famous.

There were easier ways. Write a novel. Invade a country.

Holliday stilled his warning with a hand and a smile. He had his own madness—the fearlessness of a man who was already dying. "I want to see what he's going to do with his fine guns there, and his heap of pride."

"All right then. I challenge you." He spoke calmly, but a sheen of sweat glowed on his brow.

While the two men faced each other down, Ricardo glanced at the crowd. Everyone wanted to watch—this was a story they'd tell their grandchildren, for certain. But most of them didn't want to get too close. Most held back—except for two other men, nondescript white men wearing respectable coats and laundered shirts with neat ties, boots that had seen miles, and holsters tucked away under coats. When the excitable gentleman challenged Holliday, these two each took half a step forward.

This was a trap, Ricardo was sure of it. The cowboy wouldn't be so confident if he had come here alone.

Holliday pushed back from the table. "Not even a glove to throw down. These are fallen times, aren't they?" When he flipped back the edge of his coat, a casual move meant to look like he was only straightening the garment after standing, he flashed a glimpse of his revolver. Everyone murmured. There was going to be a show.

The other two men had already left the room, ducking out by some other door in the commotion.

Holliday and his challenger marched together toward the front door like gladiators entering the arena. Not so far off, really. Ricardo took Holliday's arm and pulled him aside. "He has two friends waiting outside for you. This won't be a fair fight."

He clicked his tongue, as if disappointed but not surprised. "They never are."

"But you're still going."

"I have a reputation to maintain."

Ricardo blinked at him. "A reputation for what?"

"Surviving." He tipped his hat and winked at Ricardo, who decided he liked the man immensely.

Time was, a duelist would need a second, and Ricardo almost asked Holliday for that honor. But the lanky man marched to the middle of the street before he had a chance. Life in a young country was not so formal.

Didn't mean Ricardo couldn't do his part. He walked a little way down the street, steps crunching on dirt, and studied the surroundings. The tops of buildings, the hidden alleyways. For all his time in the West, in some of the roughest places one could ever tell tales about, Ricardo had never seen an actual gunfight. Not like this, with two faced off, hands at their sides, waiting for the draw. His heart, if he'd had one, would have been racing.

Few souls came out to watch. Most stayed indoors, crowded at windows. No one wanted to get in the way of a stray bullet. Almost no one, anyway.

He used his nose, his eyes, his other senses, listening for every heartbeat, every spot of heat moving through the world around him. And there they were, easy to spot for someone like him: one of the men had climbed to the roof of the saloon and lay flat, invisible in the darkness. He aimed down the barrel of a rifle, right at Holliday.

The other was in an alley across the street, pressed into

the shadows like his compatriot. His pistol was still holstered—he was backup, then. Holliday had three men gunning for him, not one, and it stood to reason that the one on the roof wouldn't wait for a polite count of three to fire.

The gunfighters' breath fogged in the chill night air. Ricardo's did not.

He focused everything he could feel, everything he'd learned, all that power he'd struggled to understand and fed with blood. Blood was the price for what he was, and there were rewards he'd resisted in the early days. But he'd learned to use them well.

The man on the roof breathed slow and steady, his muscles tense, and Ricardo could just about feel the tension in his trigger finger, a muscle contracting, pulling on a tendon. The man in the alley was calmer, just there to clean up whatever mess the others made. Ricardo would have to deal with him, but not first thing. With his eyes, he watched the tableau before him, Holliday and the cowboy who hadn't even had the decency to introduce himself—he likely expected to live, to be able to tell everybody the name of the man who'd shot Doc Holliday. They were a good fifty paces apart, hands at their sides, each waiting for the other to flinch. The young one looked like he stood at the edge of a volcano; Doc Holliday smiled, his skin pale with illness until it almost glowed.

Once this started, it would go quickly, but Ricardo could move faster than any of them, and he wasn't afraid. Another reward for the price he'd paid.

That trigger finger on the roof squeezed, and Ricardo stepped into the street. To observers he would look like a blur, a shadow that had detached itself from the night and somehow appeared to suddenly stand in front of Holliday. When they thought back on the moment, they would say that he had always been there—he must have come out to the street with Holliday, or maybe he had run to warn him. Something. However it happened, he was there, and the bullet from the rifle struck him.

The shot pounded into his chest and he stumbled. Three more shots fired, cracks of thunder in his ears, pounding waves of force that struck the air and brushed against his skin. Three shots, and he looked to where they came from, where he must stand so that the bullets would strike him instead of Holliday.

But all three shots had come from behind him, from Holliday.

First, the cowboy standing in front of them fell. He'd drawn, he'd gotten that far as soon as the shot rang out, but for all his bluster he was too late.

The man on the roof was next. He'd been aiming down the rifle for a second shot, probably wondering how the first had gone so far awry—obviously it had, since Holliday was still standing. But Holliday was at just the right angle to get him first. He slumped over his weapon and lay splayed on the roof as if he had dropped there from the sky.

Holliday had shot the cowboy, the man on the roof, and the one from the alley had just stepped out and raised his revolver when the last shot fired, and the man fell. He lay groaning for a short time, a strangled attempt to cry for help through blood bubbling up his throat. The sound a dying horse might make. Then he died, and that was that.

Holliday hadn't moved, merely pivoted his arm, and killed them all in less time than it took to inhale.

Ricardo touched the place on his shirt that now had a hole in it, where a little bit of blood had stained the fabric. Then he adjusted his coat to hide the spot. Holliday, replacing his gun in its holster, saw him do this but made no mention of it.

"Hey! Hey, are you all right?"

A stout man with a bushy gray mustache came running up the street. He was the sheriff, a temperance man who never set foot in the saloon, but someone must have gone to get him when trouble broke out. He grabbed Ricardo's shoulder, as if he expected him to fall over any minute now.

"I'm fine," Ricardo said. "Thank you."

"I could have sworn you got hit!"

"Just a bad angle," Ricardo said. "He missed."

"Thank goodness for that," Holliday said.

The sheriff seemed both nervous and thrilled. "I've got a dozen witnesses say that man threatened you, Holliday. Not a person here would blame you for this. If I could just get a statement—from both of you—we'll call this all finished."

Holliday had clearly done this dance before. "I'm obliged to you, sir."

They followed the sheriff back to his office.

A couple of hours later, Ricardo offered to buy Holliday a drink. They sat at a table in the corner, and after a round of excited congratulations and well wishes from the onlookers who'd witnessed the fight—and more than a few who wished they had—they were left alone.

Holliday looked exhausted. Usually, he could spend all night dealing cards and nothing more. But that little bit of effort on the street had taken a great deal out of him, and his handkerchief was spotted with blood.

"I thank you again," Holliday said. "I underestimated those jokers, and you did not."

"They thought killing you would make them famous."

"I never did get the boy's name," he said, chuckling. The sound turned to coughing, and the handkerchief covered his mouth again.

Ricardo took a deep breath and said, "I could cure you. You would live ageless, forever. There is a price. A difficult one. But you would live."

Ricardo considered that keeping alive such a man— prone to violence, expert at killing, with an attitude to suit—was perhaps not wise. Giving him the powers that came with his so-called cure was absolutely not wise, not wise at all. But more than either of those things, he thought what a shame it would be to lose him. In three hundred fifty odd years, Ricardo had never made this offer to anyone. Not even those he loved best. He wouldn't curse anyone he loved.

But this man? This man could survive very well with such a curse.

Holliday also seemed to consider, leaning back, stroking his mustache once. Ricardo couldn't guess what he was thinking. Holliday's reddened eyes gazed flatly, his expression didn't flinch—that famous poker face revealed nothing. He brought his handkerchief to his mouth and coughed, as if to emphasize his own stake in the matter.

When he drew his hand from his face, he was smiling. "I do thank you for the courtesy, sir. But to live forever in this sad world? I do not see that as a blessing."

Ricardo could be forgiven for feeling relieved.

"No, I expect to die on my feet, boots on. I'm almost looking forward to it. Better, don't you think?"

"I hadn't given it much thought," Ricardo admitted.

"What, boots?"

"Death," he said. Holliday coughed.

"You'll be off to Denver soon, then."

"Yes." He knew of a couple of bolt-holes he could use along the way. He wasn't worried. "Tomorrow night. It's time."

"I have heard—there are others like you in the city. Most of your kind stay in cities, as I understand."

"And how have you heard of such things?"

"You know of a man named Wyatt Earp?"

Ricardo smiled. "Yes. Of course I do. Just like I've heard of Doc Holliday."

Holliday tipped his hat in thanks. "Let's just say if you ever run into Mr. Earp, you watch yourself. He'll know what you are just by looking. And he doesn't much like your kind."

"Perhaps when you see him again you'll put in a good word for me."

"I don't much expect to see him again." He sounded sad. Immensely sad.

"I'm sorry. I'll watch out."

"Good."

They both looked out the window then. The reflections in the glass had faded, and the sky outside was gray.

Holliday held out his hand. "I may not see you come evening, so I'll say farewell now. You take care, sir."

Ricardo suspected that Holliday didn't much like goodbyes. Ricardo was used to them. "You as well. I'll remember you."

"That, sir, will be a kindness I do not deserve."

Holliday was dead two years later. Ricardo read about it in the papers, and that the gambler had died in bed, boots off. Ricardo mourned him and kept the story of their meeting to himself, because who would believe it? But he remembered.

EL CONQUISTADOR
DEL TIEMPO

FOR THE FIRST TIME in five hundred years, Rick stepped into a church. A real, actual, church-looking church with stone walls, stained-glass windows, carved wood statues of Mary and Joseph, cracked and age-darkened paintings of Saint Sebastian full of arrows, Saint Augustine writing his book, Daniel in the den of lions, a bearded man walking on water. But no crosses.

Vaulted ceilings arced overhead. The heart was meant to rise up, the soul filling the space as it contemplated heaven. Rick imagined that what was left of his heart and soul did so, even though this place was underground, the stained-glass windows dark, muted as a cave. He inhaled to find the air rich with stone, wax, incense, and the breath of centuries.

He didn't know the name of this church, when it had been built, why it was now buried and hidden under the Vatican. When it had been deconsecrated, to allow him and his kind to enter. He was too lost in the wonder of the moment to ask. He had never thought to return to Europe at all, and now he had seen Rome and had finally come to this ancient cathedral full of secrets.

"The Abbot is this way." The somberly dressed young woman who had guided him down the aisle gestured ahead to the transept, waiting patiently while Rick's steps slowed and his gaze traveled up and around. Young—she was at least a century old.

"Thank you," he murmured, and she left him to continue on his own. Her shoes clicked on the stone, and she disappeared into the darkness at the front of the nave.

The transept, choir, and apse had been made into a library, shelves filled with books, thousands of books, with ladders to climb to the highest of them. Scrolls filled racks, folios rested on lecterns, lying open to parchment pages only slightly yellowed with age and otherwise pristine. As in any useful library, there were desks, tables, chairs arranged for study. Enough for dozens of scholars to work here, and Rick could almost hear the rustle of turning pages, soft whispers echoing, pens scratching. A wondrous space.

Now, though, only two people were present. The curved apse was screened off to make a sort of office, lit with shaded electric lights, which seemed incongruous. The place ought to be filled with candles. Rick came to the screen, cautiously looked to the other side. Here sat a large, brown man in an enveloping monastic robe, cowl thrown back, rope belt tied loosely. His chair was upholstered in leather, padded, worn and patched many times. He did not rise but sat at the edge, hands steepled, and intently watched Rick's arrival. He was a vampire, chilled, without a heartbeat. No telling how old.

"Come forward, my son," he said.

Rick did so, glancing at the second figure present. Another vampire, this one—indeterminate, ambiguous—perched on a stool at a tall lectern, inkwell ready along with a collection of quills. They wore rather threadbare monastic robes in washed-out gray. Their head was shaved, making their jaw seem even more narrow and cheekbones even more refined. They wore an undyed silk bandage over their eyes. Rick tried not to stare, to study the mystery.

The Abbot consulted a sheet of paper, which seemed modern enough, and frowned. "You are Don Ricardo de Avila y Zacatecas, the last surviving member of Coronado's company, Conquistador de la Noche, once the Master of Santa Fe, and until last week the Master of Denver. Also called Rick." His voice was calm, his accent English, touched with unidentifiable notes.

Stunned, uncertain, Rick, Ricardo, fell back on very old habit and enacted a gesture he had not made in some three hundred years, planting his right foot, stepping back, and bending over, his hand on his heart, in a courtly bow. The movements came naturally; his body had not forgotten how to be elegant, however strange it might be to make such a bow in a modern trench coat.

"Ah," said the vampire priest. "You are one of the older ones, to be able to do that without looking like you're play-acting. But you should know that here you're just a child. Welcome to the Order of Saint Lazarus of the Shadows, Don Ricardo."

"Just Rick, please."

"We have been watching you, Ricardo."

"So I gathered. When I came here I'd hoped to learn more."

"So do we." The Abbot gestured to the figure at the lectern. The Scribe, who turned, drew a book off the shelf behind them, set it on the stand, flipped pages to the front, and smoothed out the parchment. "We have your history. We gave you your own book some time ago, when news of you started to reach us. We weren't sure at first you'd need it—most of our kind are never more than footnotes in their Masters' books, you see. But you . . . were always an odd one."

"My own book?" Rick said, wanting to laugh. "All for me? There isn't that much to tell, surely." He was staring at the shelf behind the Scribe, at all the other heavy, leather-bound books lined up. Dozens of them. Who else was written up there? Mercedes? Arturo? Alette? Yes, of course. Elinor, Catalina, Edward Alleyn, Anastasia . . . and Gaius Albinus. That was why Rick was here.

"There are some gaps we'd like to fill," the Abbot said. "You have been very mysterious, Don Ricardo."

Rick, he started to insist again, and didn't. He felt out of place here, his sense of time slipping. Maybe he shouldn't have left Denver. "I mostly tried to keep to myself."

"Please, take off your coat and sit. This may take some time. Scribe?"

Rick lay his coat over the back of a straight wooden chair and sat.

The Scribe read. Blindfolded, and they still read. Perhaps their fingers that brushed over the page were sensitive enough to feel the ink. Perhaps they had the book, and all the other books, all the histories of all vampires, memorized.

Their voice was a neutral alto, the accent flat enough

to almost be American. "In 1522 Ricardo is born in Avila, Spain, to minor nobility. Arrives in the colony of New Spain at the age of seventeen to seek his fortune, participates in Coronado's expedition to the northernmost reaches of Spanish territory. After, stays in Mexico to work as a government courier. He is thirty years old when the vampire Fray Juan finds him and turns him against his will. Ricardo manages to destroy him and his entire band."

"How?" the Abbot asked flatly. "Just a few days a vampire and you simply murder your own progenitor who possessed *centuries* of power—"

"I didn't know it couldn't be done," Rick said, ducking to hide a smile. "I had luck. Planning. Help." He'd rescued the village Fray Juan and his band preyed upon. They had been grateful. They had shown him he did not have to kill to feed and that had changed everything. "Perhaps you can tell me why it seems to happen so often that men of the cloth become . . . what we are? Or is it the other way around, that vampires become men of the cloth later?"

The Abbot leaned back. "It is easier to hide old things in the Church. Scribe?"

The Scribe had paused, finger upon the place they left off, and now continued. "In 1620 the Master of All Spain sends Mistress Catalina to rule Ciudad de México. She does not expect to find a European vampire already living in her new territory. Ricardo de Avila y Zacatecas declines the invitation to become part of Mistress Catalina's retinue."

"I've met Mistress Catalina. She would not have been happy about that."

"She was not," Rick said.

"And again, you destroyed one of the ancient, powerful vampires she sent to bring you to heel."

Rick supposed it did start to look ominous when you lined it all up like that. "Again, I had help. I gave my estancia to my human servant, Henri, so the vampires could not enter." He had always had help. Human, mortal help. He wasn't sure the Abbot would understand.

"Scribe?"

"That is in the record, reported by Mistress Catalina and her people. After, Ricardo flees north."

"Then, there is more than a century's gap in our record of you, Don Ricardo," the Abbot said.

"When is my next appearance in your book?"

"You were counted in the party of Pedro Vial that reached Saint Louis in 1792. That makes you one of the trackers who helped established the Santa Fe Trail."

The situation had been a lot more complicated than that—he had known Pedro for a long time, they ran into each other with startling frequency given the vast distances they covered. He'd only joined that particular expedition en route, when Pedro got in trouble and Rick helped him out. He hadn't thought the episode made it into any histories at all. "I worked as a tracker and translator for many of those years, yes. You see, not so interesting."

"You disappear again, until 1848."

"I moved around a lot. After 1800 or so, after the Louisiana Purchase, things in the region changed quickly. Blink of an eye. For three hundred years Spain had tried to colonize those borderlands, and in fifty years—the Anglos claimed it all. It became American."

"Why is that, do you think?"

"Spain, France, England—that land was only ever a colony to exploit. Those countries never looked on the New World as part of their own nations. Not really. But the Americans—they wanted it all. They took it. I struggled to find my place in that new country for some time."

"But you wouldn't leave."

"No. By then, it was my home."

"1848," the Abbot said.

"What about it?"

"Do you remember where you were, what you were doing?"

"As I said, I traveled—"

"Scribe?"

"Santa Fe," the Scribe said.

"Ah yes."

"You called yourself the Master of Santa Fe—for exactly one month? And that city had never had a Master before and has never had one since."

"It really was just a fluke, not really that important."

The Abbot glared. Rick ducked his gaze, cleared his throat.

"I want to know about Santa Fe."

"I keep telling you, my life, long as it has been, is not so interesting. But you, this place—I have so many questions, Abbot."

"In time. Right now I'm trying to understand *you*, Ricardo."

Now he did laugh. "Because there has been no one else like me? Is that what you're trying to tell me?"

The Abbot smiled harshly. "There has been at least one other vampire like you. One other who has lived for centuries alone, traveling, unconcerned with becoming Master of anywhere and thereby becoming Master of everywhere. Hearing your story, you remind me of Gaius Albinus."

Gaius Albinus, Dux Bellorum, was the bogeyman vampires evoked to frighten one another. Rick had met him exactly once and forced him out of Denver. The man had been hard, cold, single-minded. He promised power in exchange for obedience. It was said he would conquer the world by suborning each person in it individually. He had the time. The man carried darkness with him like a badge of honor.

"I am nothing like him."

"Are you certain?"

"You think I'm working with him. This is an interrogation." What had Rick gotten himself into? He should not have come . . .

The Abbot set aside his page of notes. "Don Ricardo. What is the most shocking thing you've ever done?"

"And now a confession? It has been five hundred years since my last—"

The Abbot waved him off. "The Order of Saint Lazarus of the Shadows forgives much. Given what we are."

"Indeed. We give God himself plausible deniability?"

"Don't blaspheme. Quickly now, first thing that comes to mind: the most shocking thing you've ever done."

He took the Abbot at his word, didn't think too hard on it, and said the first memory that came to him. "All right. I offered to Turn Doctor John Holliday."

The Scribe's pen stopped scratching. The Abbot stared. "The American gunman?"

"Yes."

"Why didn't you?"

"He refused me. I could have saved his life. He didn't want to be saved."

"Well. My goodness."

The Scribe looked at Ricardo, and he swore their eyebrows were raised under the blindfold. Then their pen once against scratched against the parchment.

"Abbot," Rick asked. "What's the most shocking thing *you've* ever done?"

"I am not the one with the blank book that needs filling," he said. But the man's gaze went soft for a moment, and he frowned deeply, caught in some dark, distant memory. Rick couldn't imagine; the possibilities defied imagination.

Clicking steps sounded on the stone aisle, and the somber young woman approached, carrying a tray with three cut-crystal glasses on it. Their contents made them gleam ruby. She reached the screened-off apse.

"Father, you said to bring refreshment."

"Yes, thank you. Set it on the desk, please." She set the tray—it was gold, polished to a shine, and likely worth thousands even disregarding any collectible or artistic value—bowed slightly, and went away. "Please, Ricardo. Drink."

He could not refuse. It wasn't just that he was hungry, that he needed to feed to stay strong and alert. This involved the most ancient rules of hospitality. When vampires invited one another to their lairs, they must provide sustenance. And the guest must accept.

The Abbot noted the hesitation. "There are mortal families connected with the Order. They voluntarily provide for us. No more than once in a month for each one. I know such details matter to you."

"Some of our kind seem to enjoy blood that tastes like fear. I never understood that."

"You prefer your blood to taste of what, generosity?"

"Kindness, I think." Maybe even love. He'd been fortunate, in those who chose to help him. There had been love.

The Abbot hauled himself from the chair. He was even taller and broader than Rick realized. In his mortal days he might have been a great warrior, swinging an ax on the battlefield, mowing down enemies. Or perhaps he had always been a monk, incongruously large in his libraries and quiet places.

The man brought one of the glasses to the lectern. The Scribe accepted with a nod, tipped the glass to their lips, drank it all down in one go. Licked their lips and took up the quill pen again. The Abbot handed a glass to Rick, then settled back in the chair with his own.

"*Ayes hugayean,*" he said, glass raised, then drank.

Rick didn't readily recognize the language, which suggested it was very old indeed. Rick sipped. The blood was still just warm and tasted sweet, tangy. Strong. The person it had come from was healthy. It made him feel a bit better. With gratitude—it might have been a prayer—he let the borrowed strength fill him.

"Better?" the Abbot asked. They all appeared more flush than they had a moment ago. Warmer. Brighter.

"Yes, thank you," Rick said.

"Now, tell me about Santa Fe."

"How do you even know about Santa Fe? I only ever passed through there, I rarely stayed—"

"Except for 1848."

"Well, yes."

"There is a footnote in the book of Catalina that says only that Elinor saw you in Santa Fe in 1848. But *she* was in Santa Fe to confront Gaius Albinus. Where did you fit into that affair? She was silent on the matter."

"By accident, I assure you."

"But you fled—"

"I did a lot of fleeing, between Zacatecas and Denver."

"And there is a century of silence around that moment. *What happened?* You met someone else there, besides Elinor. Didn't you?"

"Gaius Albinus wasn't there. I didn't meet him at all until just last year—"

"1848 in Santa Fe, Ricardo. Tell me. Begin."

His mouth opened, but he hesitated. This was an interrogation. He would tell the Abbot everything—if he knew what the man wanted to hear. At the time, the chaos of his month in Santa Fe had only seemed like chaos. What did it look like to a man who had context—millennia of history stored in those books against which to judge him?

Ricardo was five hundred years old and still managed to feel like a child much of the time. It didn't seem fair.

"All right, all right. Here is what happened in Santa Fe."

Santa Fe was on a crossroads: the road in to the mountains, to Taos, ran west. The main route of the Santa Fe Trail ran north, to the Colorado Territory and eventually to Bent's Fort, where Ricardo and Juanito were due to meet the first of the summer traders, to serve as guides and translators as they headed south. They'd stopped in Santa Fe, at the southern edge of the Sangre de Cristos, a week ago, intending to resupply and be on their way. But Juanito had fallen ill with a fever and cough. Ricardo had rented a room without windows in the back of a small adobe inn, paid extra to be left alone. And Juanito had gotten worse.

Juanito had been nineteen when Rick first met him, a wiry and brash kid convinced of his own worth and struggling to prove it to everyone else. The diminutive had made him bristle. He was sixty-five now, his hair a white fringe, his skin leathered, his joints swollen with arthritis, and he wouldn't answer to anything but Juanito.

He didn't know he was dying, but Ricardo had seen this many times. Juanito was worn out, too many miles under his feet, not enough rest. Ricardo had worn him out.

"We'll be late," Juanito said, fighting for the next breath. "They're expecting us . . . at Bent's." They'd had this conversation six nights in a row.

"It's fine," Ricardo said. "They can wait."

"I'm sure if I walk around a little, if I get in the saddle, I'll feel much better—" He tried to sit up, but a fit of coughing interrupted him. Ricardo pressed his shoulder, urging him back to the straw mattress.

"Rest, Juanito. You're very tired and should rest. Please don't worry."

Juanito settled, finally succumbing to the bed's hold. Maybe, finally, resigned. "Have you eaten yet tonight? You should eat something." He struggled to pull a sleeve back from a shaking hand, to expose his wrist.

Ricardo tugged the sleeve back in place. "You're too weak right now to provide."

"I'm not. I'm *not*." A spark of that brash nineteen-year-old shone through. His breath rattled.

Ricardo looked away, squeezed shut his eyes against tears. This feeling in his chest, where his heart would be breaking if he still had a living heart, was also familiar. Nothing to do but march forward through it.

"Juanito. Rest."

The man's breathing deepened into sleep but still rattled in a way that seemed to echo through his whole chest. Ricardo fled, just for a moment, to the courtyard at the front of the inn and then outside, to get some air that wasn't filled with illness, to walk out some of his grief. Outside smelled of pines and piñons, and he cleared his lungs, refreshed himself.

The matron of the house, Imelda Constance, stopped at the doorway. "How is your friend?" Ricardo shook his head, and the matron crossed herself.

He asked, "Is there a surgeon nearby? He needs a doctor—"

"No surgeon," she said. "But I will bring Santa Lucinda."

"Santa Lucinda?" That seemed a bit presumptuous, but one didn't argue with nicknames.

"The curandera."

"I'm not sure—"

"I trust Lucinda. I will send for her and all will be well, you'll see."

"But he needs a doctor," Ricardo murmured. Imelda was already at the gate, yelling at one of the stable boys to carry a message.

The house was close enough to the plaza to hear traffic outside, even at night. Travelers arriving after nightfall, townsfolk out for drinks and dinner or other entertainments. A tune from an idly strummed guitar carried. This was a good place to be. A good place to rest for a while. Since he had to, he was glad it was here. He had to be at peace with this; he had no choice.

He went back to the room for the long vigil. Juanito might linger for a week or be gone in an hour. Ricardo would be by his side, however long it took. The room was smoky, too hot in the thick air. He didn't need to breathe, so the sourness of the sick room didn't touch him. Still, his nerves thrummed, a tension running up to him like the hoofbeats of an approaching cavalry. He did not know if it was the waiting or if Juanito was right and he needed to eat.

Later. He could feed later.

A commotion sounded in the courtyard, two women calling greetings and exchanging a rush of news. Her expression alight, Imelda appeared outside the sickroom a moment later.

"Here she is, Santa Lucinda!"

Ricardo stood to greet the woman coming up behind Imelda. She was taking off her shawl, which the matron accepted from her reverently. The curandera's dark-colored dress was clean, simple. Her black hair lay down her back in a braid. She was young—couldn't have been much more than twenty. Ricardo didn't know why he'd expected an old woman, but her unlined face, shining eyes, surprised him. And she was pregnant, maybe six months along. He could hear the baby's heartbeat.

He caught her gaze, and they stared at one another a moment. He couldn't see through her, couldn't sense a thing from her. Usually, he looked in a person's eyes, and he could drive his will into them, persuade them, speak and have them obey without effort. She was like a wall, and her lips turned in the smallest of smiles, as if she knew this. She was unafraid.

Then her gaze broke off. She looked him up and down, shook her head. "I cannot help you. Your curse cannot be lifted."

"Yes, I know—" He blinked a moment, uncertain who'd been trying to cast a spell on whom. "It's not for me, it's my friend. Please." He stepped aside and gestured her into the room. She gave a quick, determined nod—this, she could do.

Pulling the strap of a canvas bag off her shoulder, she went straight to the bed and knelt. She surveyed the sick man in a businesslike manner, touching both his wrists, his throat. Using her thumbs to gently open his eyes.

"His name is Juanito," Ricardo said worriedly. He tried to trust her.

Juanito's lips worked, but he may or may not have been aware of what was happening. Lucinda drew back the blanket, exposing his too-thin frame, the worn cotton shirt hanging too loosely over it, and watched the rise and fall of his chest.

"I need hot water," she said to Imelda, who lingered at the doorway. The matron rushed to the kitchen. The curandera drew out a series of items from her bag—many items. It had not seemed so full, hiding its bulk well. A copper bowl, a clay cup, a handful of kindling for a fire, a bundle of sage, a series of pouches that smelled like a garden.

"Can you help him?" Ricardo asked, too eagerly.

Lucinda stood, grabbed the front of his shirt, and pulled him into the hallway. Softly she said, "He is at the end of his time. I can make him more comfortable, that is all."

Ricardo rubbed his eyes. Even now, he had hoped. After all this time, he still hoped.

"You must have known this," she said, frowning. "You must have seen this before, you who stand on the threshold of death at every moment."

"How would you know that? What do you see, when you look at me?"

"I see a shadow." Her brow furrowed. "Who are you? Where exactly do you come from?"

"I'm not sure you really want those answers."

Scowling, she turned back to Juanito. In moments the room was filled with wisps of burning sage. Imelda arrived with a kettle of water, just finished boiling, and set it on a side table in the room. Lucinda worked over it with quick, deft hands, reaching past her round belly to take pinches out of little bags, add them to the cup, fill it with water. Whispering words over it. Ricardo had no idea what she spoke, what any of the substances were. But Juanito drank down the liquid as he hadn't consumed anything in days. His breath stopped rattling quite so much.

"There, breathe, my friend," Lucinda said, stroking back Juanito's hair. When he seemed like he slept, she rounded her shoulders, put a hand on the small of her back, and sighed. Gave Ricardo another hard look.

"You could save him," she said.

"Would that really be saving? No."

"Well, isn't that something?" She worked to stand, leaning on the bed, hefting her weight upright. Ricardo was too late to help her and contritely looked at his feet while she settled into a chair in a corner and drew some knitting from her bag. Ricardo sat in his usual chair at the bedside.

They waited. Always the waiting. Maybe Juanito would hold on for another day. Maybe he would pass while Ricardo slept out the daylight hours. He hoped not; he wanted to be there. To witness.

"Ricardo. You still haven't eaten," the soft voice came from the bed.

"I told you not to worry about me."

Grumbling, Juanito settled back against the pillow.

"This way, this way . . ." Imelda's voice carried down the hallway. Two sets of footsteps approached, and then a man in a black cassock, wooden cross hung prominently around his neck, appeared in the doorway.

Ricardo leapt from the chair, hands clenched. "We did not call for a priest!"

Eyes wide, the priest stepped back, straight into Imelda, who pleaded, "But señor, your friend, I only thought—"

"You!" The priest had managed to get a look at the room, past Ricardo, who was trying to block his way while avoiding coming close to that cross. Ricardo looked at where the priest pointed angrily—at Lucinda.

"Yes, me!" she said, grinning. "How are you, padre?"

"Señora Imelda, I can't be in the same room with that *woman*."

"But Father, this man is very ill, and you know Santa Lucinda knows better than anyone how to comfort the sick—"

"She isn't a saint!" the priest declared.

"Out, both of you, out." Ricardo crowded the doorway and herded them into the hall. "Imelda, I did not ask for a priest."

"Yes, but under the circumstances . . ."

"Señor, I am Father Diego, and you are?" He was slender,

his hair shaved into a thin tonsure. The crow's-feet at his eyes were faint. He seemed very earnest.

"Not overly fond of priests."

"I am sorry to hear that. Perhaps we could speak together. You could come to the chapel for confession—"

Ricardo laughed. "I'm sorry, I'm not trying to be harsh. But you're not welcome here."

"Ricardo!" Imelda said, aghast. "Your friend should see a priest!" Diego nodded, head bobbing like a bird's.

Ricardo managed not to yell. Took a breath so he'd have enough air to speak with. "Can you wait here a moment?"

The sick room no longer smelled as sour as it had. Sage, herbs, steam—a comfortable warmth instead of a sticky heat. Lucinda sat quietly, wholly involved in her knitting. Giving Ricardo and Juanito space, and peace. He knelt by the bed.

"Juanito," he said softly. When his friend's eyes opened, Ricardo didn't know whether to feel relieved or disappointed. He wanted his friend's pain to end. And he didn't want his friend to leave. "A priest is here. If you want to see him, I'll show him in. If you don't, I'll send him away."

Juanito nodded, and his voice scratched. "Maybe . . . maybe I should see the priest. Ricardo . . . when I confess my sins, I will not tell him about you."

"You consider me one of your sins?" Ricardo said, smiling, and Juanito chuckled.

"No, no, not like that. But I do not think a priest will understand you."

Ricardo touched his arm. "You should tell him whatever you need to be at peace. Don't worry about me."

The priest was waiting in the hall with Imelda, who was

wringing her hands.

"Juanito will see you, Father." Ricardo stepped aside.

It was likely Ricardo's imagination that the priest nodded smugly at him. Imelda turned her gaze skyward and whispered a prayer. Ricardo left them both and went to the courtyard. The house had become rather crowded.

Midnight was coming on; the streets had emptied, the lanterns put out. In the dark, the stars blazed in the desert sky. The same stars he'd always seen, so at least that was a comfort. He could stay in one place and the world would move on around him, but the stars didn't care.

Lucinda came into the courtyard then, stepping softly, wrapping her shawl tight over her shoulders. He glanced at her, then back to the sky.

"Got tired of Father Diego giving you that look?" he asked her.

"Diego and I have known each other for years, he can't get rid of me so easily. I just needed fresh air, like you." He didn't need air at all, really, but he nodded. "I have only known him an hour, but I think your friend Juan is a good man."

"One of the best," Ricardo said. "And I have known many good men."

"Do you have him under a spell or did he choose this path?"

"Did he choose to follow a demon like me, is what you mean?" He shook his head. "I'm not sure. I'm never sure. I tell myself that they choose to stay with me. Then I decide they're just being nice and I should send them away. But it turns out I like having friends."

"You're very strange."

"I hear that a lot."

"How old are you, demon?"

He chuckled. "I was once told never to say my age. But that was a long time ago—"

Just then a man came to the courtyard gate and paused, hand on the adobe wall, looking in. He pursed his lips, seemed to make a decision, and stepped in, nodding politely at both Ricardo and Lucinda. He appeared to be in his thirties, weathered and strong. Skin like burnished sandstone. One of the indigenous peoples, but not local. He wore a cotton shirt, a wool jacket over it, wool trousers and worn boots, a couple of cords of beads around his neck, a band of cloth around his head, pressing back his black hair.

He approached Ricardo and spoke a rapid staccato of a language Ricardo didn't know.

"That's Navajo," Lucinda said. "Do you know it?"

He shook his head and tried a couple of languages he did know. Pueblo, and the man shook his head. Then, Apache. "I don't speak your tongue. Can you understand me?"

"Yes," the man answered in Apache. "I'm looking for El Conquistador. Are you him?"

Ricardo felt a vague foreboding. He tried so hard to remain unnoticed, to avoid attention. Didn't seem to be working. "Yes, I suppose I am."

"You're in danger. You and everyone around you."

He supposed he should have expected that.

"How many languages do you speak?" the Abbot interrupted.

Rick needed a moment to respond, his narrative disrupted; his memories had taken him to a far-off place.

"How many do I speak now? Or how many have I ever spoken? Spanish, of course, a bit of Latin and French. Some Nahuatl. I've lost much of the Apache, I'm afraid, and the Pueblo, though I'm picking it back up again. The Internet has been wonderful for practicing languages. I never did learn much Navajo, but I spoke passable Lakota Sioux. The English came relatively recently." One of those vast, quick changes. In only a hundred years, English became the language he spoke most.

"But it's such an odd smattering," the Abbot said. "All of it so . . . local."

"It was what I needed. I was a guide and translator on the Santa Fe Trail. What else was I supposed to speak?"

"Is it true that you never once returned to Europe?"

"It's true. I never even went east of the Mississippi, except for a trip to New Orleans."

"Why did you stay in that part of the world?" the Abbot asked, and the Scribe's pen scratched.

Rick said, "Have you studied what modern medicine has discovered about human blood?"

"Science has little to do with our kind," the Abbot said, sniffing.

"At higher altitudes, the air is thinner. The blood develops more blood cells, to better carry oxygen. Some athletes train at high altitude, to strengthen their blood's efficiency. The blood there becomes richer. So. In the Rocky Mountains and high desert in the southwest of the North American continent, our kind requires less blood to survive."

The Scribe's pen stopped, and they stared at Rick. The Abbot's mouth opened, disbelieving.

"You're making that up," he said.

Ricardo shrugged. "I also like the scenery. There's enough space to hide."

They exchanged names, or tried to. The Navajo man said, "Call me John."

Ricardo chuckled. "Is that really your name?"

"It's what you can call me." He was a medicine man, he said. A monster slayer, though Ricardo wasn't sure he understood the concept correctly. There was a term in there that didn't translate, he suspected. Maybe what he meant was closer to a spy? Whatever he was, he had one foot in the supernatural world and kept track of the dangers lurking there. Like vampires.

Lucinda offered the man a drink. He accepted water, and they sat on a wooden bench in the courtyard, among pots of herbs and flowers, under the stars.

"What exactly is going to happen?" Ricardo asked John.

"Santa Fe is at a crossroads," he said.

"Yes, I know—"

"Not just in space but in time. If I knew exactly what would happen I would stop it myself."

"What do you expect me to do?"

"Not sure. But it's your people who bring the threat. You know them, the rest of us don't."

The rest of us. The natives, the settlers, the medicine men, the curanderos and curanderas. All the traditions that had grown up without the rule of vampires lurking beneath them. He was the only vampire in this part of the world. At least he'd thought so.

"The Families are moving into Santa Fe," Ricardo said.

"Is that it? The Santa Fe Trail, the migration from America—it's opening territory to them that hasn't been available before." There hadn't been enough people in the West, concentrated in enough cities, to support more than a few solitary vampires. That was changing. This man had felt it. Ricardo—he hadn't wanted to admit it.

"So you do understand," the medicine man said. "The stories of El Conquistador say you are a monster but that you help people. I thought you'd like some warning of what's coming. So you can help."

"Dammit," Ricardo muttered and scrubbed his scalp, mussing his hair.

"What did he say?" Lucinda asked in Spanish.

"He suspects the whole region is about to be overrun with demons like me, and he expects me to do something about it."

She thought for a moment, then said, "And will you?"

"I can't protect my own friends, much less the town, or the whole territory," Ricardo replied in Spanish, then said the same in Apache.

John seemed unsympathetic. "At least you have some warning now. We didn't have any warning, the first time you came here."

"You mean 'you' as in 'you people.' Not me personally."

"You're called El Conquistador for a reason, aren't you?"

What exactly did the people telling these stories think they knew about him? That first expedition had been an army with swords and arquebuses, totally mundane weapons. No—wholly supernatural to a people who didn't have forged steel and gunpowder. A troop of vampires might be less frightening. Stopping them wasn't impossible. Just difficult.

Ricardo gazed skyward. "So what, I need to start teaching everyone how exactly to kill me?" He ought to leave. He was supposed to be riding to Bent's Fort by now, with Juanito. This wasn't his responsibility.

John looked out over the courtyard's low wall. "Someone's coming."

Ricardo felt it the next moment: a chill, a tension in the air like lightning about to strike. No, not this, not now. He didn't want to deal with it. It had been decades since he'd chanced upon another demon like himself, another vampire. New Orleans, back in 1790. There had been far too many vampires in New Orleans, and they had all wanted to see him, to speak with him, as if he was some kind of legend. El Conquistador, who had been in the Americas a century longer than any other of their kind. Ricardo had explained himself as little as possible and then left. Vampires were exhausting.

"They're here," he said to John. Then in Spanish, "Lucinda, don't let anyone in the house. If anyone comes here wanting to be invited in—do not invite them. Not anyone. Keep everyone inside. Do you understand?"

"Yes, but—"

Ricardo went out into the street, tracking the chill that spiked the air.

Imelda's house was a few streets away from the plaza, but the main road leading to the center of town ran close by, and it was here Ricardo encountered a troop of twelve men on horseback. Five of them were vampires, the rest human, leading packhorses, carrying weapons. They were dusty, sweaty, as if they had been on a long journey.

Standing in the middle of the road, Ricardo waited. They must have sensed him. Would they be surprised? The troop came to a shuffling, disorganized stop. Yes, they were surprised. Hands tightened on reins, touched weapons.

"Who are you?" the leader of the troop called. A woman. One of the other riders had a crossbow in hand, a wooden bolt loaded. Ah yes, he would be careful.

"I am Ricardo de Avila," he said.

"*Ricardo?* Dios, you're still alive?" She dismounted. The woman wore trousers and a buckskin jacket. Her thick hair was tied back in a tail and tucked under a bowler cap.

Ricardo stared. "Elinor?" She was a beautiful woman, and he'd admired her the first time they met. Two hundred years ago was it? That seemed outrageous, but here they were.

"Elinor was alone?" The Abbot interrupted, again. Rick was more than willing to tell his story, but he wanted to get it over with. This was taking much longer than it needed.

"No, she had an entourage, a few younger vampires, lieutenants and such, human servants. People like her are never alone."

"Anyone of note? Anyone older than her?" he asked, with an urgency that seemed out of place. This had happened almost two hundred years ago. What could it matter now?

"No, no one. At least not that I could tell. They all deferred to her. What are you trying to learn, Sir Abbot? What mystery about me are you trying to solve with these questions?"

"I'm only trying to draw out the complete story—"

"No. Then you would simply let me tell it. This is more. If you just tell me what you need to know—"

"And have you tell me what you think I want to hear? Oh no. Tell the story, Don Ricardo."

Her smile seemed pleased. "You remember me! I'm glad."

"How are you?"

"I have to admit, I'm a little stunned. What are you doing here?"

"I was going to ask the same thing," he said. "Could you perhaps ask your man there to lower the weapon? I know how slippery the triggers can be on those things."

"Xander, it's fine," she said over her shoulder, and the man—who appeared young but that meant nothing—lowered the crossbow. Didn't put it away, though. Hand on her hip, she considered Ricardo, her gaze narrowed. He knew better than to look into her eyes. The lock of hair framing her cheek was enough.

"You've been traveling," Ricardo said. "When did you leave Ciudad de México?"

"It's been a while," she said. "Ricardo, tell me what you're doing here in Santa Fe. Be specific." She sounded urgent. Panicked even, if he didn't know better.

Ricardo decided to tell the truth. "My friend is dying. I've only stopped here to witness his passing."

"Your friend," she said, as if she couldn't believe him having one. "You could save him."

"Saving. Why does everyone call it saving when they know better?"

"Are there any other of our kind in town? In the region?"

"Not that I know of. Are you looking for someone?"

She glared. Yes, she was.

"It's none of my concern," Ricardo said quickly. "I'm only curious."

"You've met no one?" she said. "You're still solitary, even after all this time? You should be ruling this territory by now."

He chuckled softly. He'd heard this before. "I only want to be left alone. Myself and my friends, that is."

"I don't believe you."

He shrugged, using his whole arms. "I can't help that."

"Ricardo. The Master of Spain has been overthrown. La Reina Catalina has declared independence from his successor and will not defer to him. And now Dux Bellorum is coming, to occupy the territory to the north in an effort overcome her."

War, Elinor was speaking of war. Was such a thing—a war between vampires—normal? Common, even?

"What . . . who is Dux Bellorum?" Ricardo asked.

She laughed. "How can you be three hundred years old and still such a ninny? You really haven't heard of Dux Bellorum, in all your years?"

"No."

She hesitated a moment, then repeated, "I don't believe you."

He almost walked away but for his suspicion that this was about to get ugly and he still didn't know enough.

"This Dux Bellorum—he's here?" Ricardo asked. "Or he's coming here. And you come to make war on him. Is that right?"

"How can you not know this?"

"Because I don't care to! Leave me out of it. I do not know this Dux Bellorum, I want nothing to do with him or you."

"You won't have a choice! If he hasn't already found you, he will, and he will demand that you serve him or he will kill you!"

This just made him tired. "He frightens you. You're terrified!"

"Dux Bellorum is the monster that vampires tell stories about to frighten one another. He means to conquer us all and unite us under his banner. To hold all our power for himself."

Rick chuckled. "Like what, some Alexander the Great of vampires? Master of all? Why?"

"Why not? What else should he do with his time?"

"Good night, Elinor. Good night to all of you. I will not interfere in whatever war you have brought to Santa Fe, and do not expect me to participate. Good night." He gave them a mock bow, doffing an imaginary cap, and walked away.

"Ricardo!" Elinor called after him, but he did not stop.

He also did not go straight back to Imelda's. Instead, he went in the opposite direction, turned down a couple of stray corners, and found a shadow to wait in, to see if he was followed. And he was, by one of those strong young vampires who rode in Elinor's train. They might have been her own progeny, made to serve her. Ricardo didn't breathe, kept himself stiller than death, quieter than darkness, in the shadow of an adobe wall. The man likewise traveled silently in shadow; Ricardo never would have seen him if he hadn't been watching. But each sensed the other, that hard chill of the undead tainting the air.

The man, a stony look in his dark eyes, dark hair curling around his ears, had a wooden stake. From a distance the long pole carried at his side looked like a rapier blade, but it was made to kill vampires. He was stealthy, quiet. He kept to the same shape as the shadows around him. But he was not as old or as strong as Ricardo.

Ricardo had heard stories that vampires could disappear, travel as mist, turn into bats, appear out of thin air. In truth, he simply moved very, very quickly, and so silently that no hunting dog would sense him. He didn't go far—he wanted his tracker to stay where he was, to think he still had Ricardo in his sights. At the house next door, Ricardo found what he was looking for in a pile of firewood. A broken stick, with enough of a sharp end to be a threat. He wouldn't have to make noise by breaking it. Moving like the night air itself, he slipped out of the house's yard, up the street, and put the man in his sights.

Elinor should have known better, sending just one man against him. He paused, searched again, sensing for that particular chill in the air, and yes, it was just the one man. Elinor and the others had moved away. With his target squarely in sight, Ricardo rushed from the wall to the stand of trees where the man waited, slipping behind him before he recognized the danger. He planted the sharp end of the stake at his back and murmured close to his ear.

"Does Elinor think so little of me that she only sent you, or does she think so little of you that she would sacrifice you?"

The man flinched and stiffened, as if the stake had already gone through him. Ricardo only held it there, so if the man tried to move he would impale himself.

"I swear I was only sent to watch you, to see where you went and who you spoke with. I swear!"

"Your weapon is in your hand as if you mean to use it."

"It's dangerous here!"

"Indeed."

"Please señor, I was only sent to watch, I promise."

"And perhaps kill me if you saw the opportunity?" The man might have whimpered a little. "Tell Elinor to leave me alone. Understand?" He poked the stick a little harder. Not enough to break through the wool of his jacket. But enough to make him nervous.

"Yes . . . yes, señor."

"Good." Ricardo stepped back, let the man turn to face him. He was young, handsome. Just a boy. He probably thought he was so strong, so powerful. "You should go back to Elinor. Don't follow me, yes?"

He nodded quickly. Licked his lips. "Is . . . is it true that you rode with Coronado? That you were the first vampire in all of Mexico?"

Ricardo sighed, looked heavenward. "Yes, I rode with Coronado. No, I was not the first. I killed the first. Remember that."

He shoved him, and the man ran but pulled up short. He had sensed what Ricardo had in the same moment, a new presence approaching. This was different than the vampires' chill; it was dark and carried the charge of violence. Ricardo didn't recognize it.

"What is that?" Ricardo said.

The man's gaze went wide, trembling. His body seemed like it might break with tension. "Dux Bellorum, he is here!"

"No, this isn't a vampire, it's different. Listen!" Ricardo jogged out to the middle of the street to see.

A streak of movement caught his eye, something low and fast. He narrowed his gaze, focused, but it was gone. Then came another following the first, a low, furry creature running across the road some distance ahead. Ricardo got a decent look when it stopped and glanced back at him: a wolf, huge, bulky, gray-and-black fur bristling all over. Its open mouth showed large, yellowing teeth. Their gazes met, just for a moment, before the creature dashed off.

"Wolf men," his erstwhile companion said. Still afraid. "Dux Bellorum's army. I must go warn Doña Elinor." He vanished in speed and shadow, leaving Ricardo with whatever approached.

Wolf men?

"This was the first time you'd encountered werewolves, then?" the Abbot asked.

"European-derived werewolves, yes. The native peoples have magicians, shape-shifters, skin-walkers, other sorts of wolf folk and creatures. They're not the same things."

"Are the European sort more or less dangerous?"

"Yes," Rick said, his smile sly. "May I continue?"

"Please."

Ricardo had left his pistol back at the inn. Not that he was sure it would do him any good. What were these wolf men? More important, what stopped them?

The two wolves were the advance guard for a gang of

horsemen who followed. The road under his feet shook with the approaching thunder of hoofbeats, a disconcerting sound in the middle of the night, especially since it was the second such encounter. Ricardo waited.

Eight horses crowded in, wearing saddlebags packed for a journey, and eight riders done up with hats, dusters, boots, pistols and rifles, for a long ride where they might find trouble. The horses were nervous, tossing their heads, their ears pinned back. All of them unhappy and showing it, stamping and dancing, doing small battle with their riders at every step, and the riders yanking on the reins and sitting back hard, trying to ride through it. The horses were sweating, spooked. Horses and wolves generally didn't get along, and these were being forced to. That was what it looked like to Ricardo.

The lead rider spotted him, reined his horse back, and his company followed suit. A quiet standoff ensued as they regarded each other. Ricardo hadn't even put his coat on when he left the house. He was in shirtsleeves, in the same trousers he'd been wearing all week. At least he had his boots on. He tried to stand at ease, wearing a friendly smile, as if he greeted friends. Trusted that he'd be able to dodge if they tried to kill him.

The two large wolves settled on the side of the street, a bit behind him—he had to turn his head to get a good look at them. The creatures glared, hackles stiff.

Ricardo looked each of the men over. A couple of gringos, the others of indeterminate mixed race. The white man who rode in front dressed finely, with a burgundy vest and long duster, a thick ring on the hand that rested on his thigh. He must have been the leader.

"Buenas noches, señores," Ricardo said.

The leader laughed, but the sound was forced, uncertain. "Who are you?" His English was flat American.

"Just a traveler passing through. I'm not looking for trouble." In those days, he spoke English with a thick Spanish accent. The language tasted awkward to him.

"Pete, he's a vampire," one of the other riders hissed.

"Yes, I know that."

"He's not one of ours!"

"Shut up!"

Amused, Ricardo said, "This is an unusual company to be traveling through this region."

"Is it, now? Might say the same for you."

"I expect so."

"Boss'll want to talk to him," the chatty one said.

"Quiet!"

"Pete, is it?" Ricardo said. "What is it you mean to do here in Santa Fe?"

"Stick around, you'll find out."

"And where is this . . . boss of yours?" Was this who Elinor warned him about? Dux Bellorum?

"Come with us. We'll take you to him." The leer on his face was wolfish.

"No. If he wants to speak with me, he'll come find me."

Pete narrowed his gaze, considering. "You're El Conquistador, aren't you? Heard stories."

Why was it everyone had heard these stories but him? "That's very flattering."

"I think you should come with us." This was spoken with the inflection of a threat. It seemed Ricardo's reputation made him a challenge. A trophy.

"I will not."

The leader of the wolf men drew and fired the pistol from his belt in almost the same motion.

The impact hit Ricardo's right shoulder, and he stumbled back.

The wolves sprang next, from both sides.

Pain seared through his shoulder, but Ricardo put that aside for now and moved with all the speed and power of his cursed existence. The wolves were supernatural as well, stronger and faster than they looked. But not like him. He became shadow. Time slowed, and his attackers became sluggish to his eyes. He expected them, knew where they would be, could step around them as easily as moving around furniture. To them, he would have become a blur. They'd lose sight of him. The darker one came at him first, from his right. Before they could track his movements, Ricardo pivoted, then again, getting behind the dark wolf, grabbing him under a foreleg, hauling up—and throwing.

The other had likely hoped to flank him, pen him in while the other pinned him and mauled. Then their master would come and drain his blood, taking all those centuries of power for himself. This did not happen.

Ricardo slammed the first wolf to the ground. The second yelped and scrambled back to get out of his partner's way, but Ricardo had already moved again, so fast the air felt warm against his skin, and he grabbed this second wolf by the scruff of his neck. No more difficult than taking hold of a large puppy. Baring his teeth, Ricardo reveled in the power. He yanked back the wolf's head, pulling his front half off the ground, immobilizing him. Ricardo could break his neck with a twist. Probably wouldn't kill him, but it would stop him for a while. The wolf's rib cage pressed against Ricardo's arms, and the creature gasped for breath. The other had got back on his feet and stood growling but kept his distance. He slammed the second wolf to the ground as well. Yelping, he backed away. Ricardo rubbed his shoulder where the bullet had hit him. Blood spattered the white fabric, but not a lot.

The horses before him shifted, blew out nervous breaths, expressing their riders' anxiety. All the men had gone still, staring at him. They had not expected this.

Ricardo said, "You might ask yourself how a vampire survives alone for as long as I have before thinking you can destroy him so easily."

If he had been alone, he could have fought them all. Moved fast as wind, pulled them all from their horses and slammed them to the ground, broken their necks. They were supernatural; this alone might not have killed them. But they'd certainly have been surprised. But Ricardo was not alone, and Juanito was dying in a house a few streets away. Others with Juanito were vulnerable. They were Ricardo's primary concern. And so he fled. There was shouting as the horses spooked. A wolf howled; Ricardo heard their claws scraping in the dirt as they followed, but he quickly lost them. He took a roundabout route, running along a tangled path of streets and plazas, circling back, ensuring he was not followed, until he approached Imelda's house. He waited some time, testing the air, making sure he was alone. And he was.

They would likely tell stories about him. More stories.

The waxing moon had not moved all that far across the sky. The adventures with Elinor and the pack of wolf men had not taken more than half an hour. John was still in the courtyard, sitting on the bench, his hands cupped around a mug of steaming drink.

"Is everyone all right?" Ricardo asked urgently. "Has anyone come to the house?"

"Do you know you've been shot?" he asked, nodding at the hole in his shirt, spotted with red.

"Yes. Answer my question."

"A woman came," John said. "Young, good-looking. She asked to come in and I said no."

"Good. You were right—the war has already come to Santa Fe. Where is Lucinda?"

"She's gone to see your friend. He's not doing well."

Ricardo nodded and went straight in. When he reached Juanito's room, he nearly collapsed next to the bed. His vision swam until he paused, collected himself, and focused on his friend.

"What's that on your shirt?" Lucinda asked. She sat on the other side of the bed, kettle in one hand and cup of steaming infusion in the other. Father Diego sat in the back chair, a wood bead rosary laced around his fingers. Imelda stood at this side, clasping her own rosary tightly.

"It's nothing," he said.

"You've been shot!"

"Everyone says that as if I don't already know," Ricardo said, his voice low, threatening. A rage was building in him.

Juanito knew immediately what was wrong. "You're weak. I told you." His voice was barely a whisper, and he could no longer raise his head from the pillow. "You need to drink."

Ricardo had done too much, used too much of his

strength. He had already gone several nights without feeding. He was strong, yes, but his power needed blood. His power was hungry.

"Santa Fe has become interesting, you might say," Ricardo said.

"Oh no," the ill man sighed.

"What's wrong?" Lucinda asked. They all looked at Ricardo expectantly.

"Santa Fe is at a crossroads," he sighed. "But that isn't important right now. How are you?" He put a hand on his friend's arm.

"I'm dying."

Ricardo bowed his head, almost so his chin touched his chest. "I wish you wouldn't say that."

"But it's true. You can't help me. But all these people? Whatever is happening in this town? Help them."

He supposed he could take it as the man's dying wish.

Ever since he'd been cursed, he'd known the world was filled with strangeness and terrors. He had tried to live a good life despite it all. Not let the power overcome him. And certainly not let anyone who desired such power use him. Now the battle had come to him.

He had an idea.

"I will need all your help," he said to the others in the room. "Let us go out to the courtyard to talk. Juanito, I'll be back soon."

"I'll be here."

Imelda, Lucinda, and Father Diego followed him to the courtyard, where John was standing, looking out over the wall. The priest clutched his beads even more tightly; his hands were shaking.

"Señor," Diego said. "You have been shot, you should lie down, the señora should tend your wound—"

"You see, Padre, I'm no longer even bleeding." Ricardo tugged at the ruined corner of his shirt, the single hole only marked with a spattering of blood. He should have been drenched, but he no longer even felt pain.

"¡Dios!" Diego quickly backed away, crossed himself so fast his hand seemed to tangle with itself. He ran into the courtyard wall.

"You see, there are worse things than healer women," Ricardo murmured.

"What are you?" the priest cried out.

John seemed amused and looked the priest up and down as if he found the man wanting. "He's called El Conquistador. He's lived three hundred years. A monster of the dark. But he has many friends, so who's to say what he is?"

They were all staring at Ricardo now. One thing to say he was some indeterminate and perhaps inconsequential demon. Another thing to have it laid out so clearly.

"He pays the rent in advance," Imelda said, shrugging, as if the practical consideration stood for all.

"Shh," the Navajo man said. "Hear that?"

A howling voice filled the night—the piercing, drawn-out call of a wolf. Then another, and another. All from different directions, as if they surrounded the plaza.

"Wolves in the city?" Father Diego said. "I've never heard them so close."

"They're not wolves, not really," Ricardo said.

"What is happening?" Lucinda demanded, her hands laced over her belly.

"The demons have come to Santa Fe, Father. All those

stories that the priests frightened us with when we were children—they're all of them true."

"And you're one of them! If demons are in Santa Fe, it's because you have brought them!"

"Oh, there's so much worse than I in the world," Ricardo said. "Men who are wolves, women who drink blood, beings who can't be killed, who come out at night—they are here in Santa Fe and preparing to do battle." And what awful timing for Ricardo to be here in the middle of it. He sometimes felt he had spent most of his three hundred years fleeing from these battles, and now they were catching up to him.

Imelda was praying audibly now. Lucinda was also praying, words that flowed like a chant, and she sprinkled herbs from a pocket in her dress all around the courtyard.

"And you would save us from these monsters?" Diego said, voice edging to panic. "You cannot! You are cursed! You have no soul, you are damned!"

"Yes. Probably. My soul was taken from me through no fault of my own. What of that? What of God's forgiveness, then? If I have no soul, if I am already damned, than what is left to me but my choices? So I choose to do good and hope for salvation no matter how hopeless it seems. Would you have me do otherwise, Father Diego? Would you hear my confession now and take it as I offer it, in earnest?" If a demon repents, does one believe it? Ricardo didn't need Diego to trust him. Just . . . not interfere.

The wolf howl came again, joined by a second, and a third. A chorus that sounded like a battle cry.

"How do we stop them?" Lucinda asked.

"I have an idea—"

Diego said, "The strength of the Lord our God will be enough to save us, if we all pray together—"

They didn't have time for this. "Padre, yes, the Lord our God is strong, I don't dispute this. But believe me when I say that it won't be enough. And I need your help. Will you help?"

"I . . . I . . ."

Ricardo went on. "Some of these demons cannot enter consecrated spaces. Churches are forbidden to them. Can you consecrate as much of the city as you can? You see, a simple thing, it will not taint your soul at all. It is God's work. Start at the plaza, the church. Work your way out. Protect as much space as you can—but keep some of the streets clear. Here." He found a stick, a patch of ground, began scratching out a map of the plaza and the surrounding area. "This stretch here." He pointed out the main road leading out of town, and the branch that led to the plaza in one direction and the western foothills in the other. "Keep this space unconsecrated, profane. Do you understand?"

"Because by keeping this road clear . . . you'll funnel our enemies to the space you control. A bottleneck."

"Exactly!"

"This will keep us safe," he said wonderingly. "But you—"

"Don't worry about me," Ricardo said and then explained it all again to John in Apache.

"This won't stop the wolf men," John said.

"That's where I need you and Lucinda to help. Every protection spell you know, every charm and incantation, every talisman and totem. Bring them all. Everyone you know who practices such magic, get their help. Surround the city if you can." And again in Spanish for Lucinda and the others. He tried to be patient. He was losing words, mixing languages. He had to be clear.

"It's blasphemy—" the priest started, and Ricardo glared.

"We need all the help we can get—"

"Ricardo! Ricardo de Avila, I need to speak with you! If the mistress of the house won't invite me in, you must come out here!" Elinor was shouting from outside the courtyard wall.

"If you'll excuse me a moment," he said, bowing slightly, and went to the gate to look out. She stood in the street, again surrounded by her entourage. The poor young man she had sent to spy on him was there, looking ruffled.

They smelled of blood, a tangy-sweet aura that clung to them, though their clothing was clean, though they had sucked every drop of it off their teeth. Ricardo's muscles clenched, his nerves fired. He yearned toward that smell, swayed on his feet for just a second. But that was too much. Showed too much weakness. He was determined to hold himself strong, to stay within the protection of Imelda's house as he glared out.

"Buenas noches, Elinor," he said.

"Ricardo. I understand you've had a busy night."

"Indeed, and it keeps getting busier. What do you want?"

"You've met the werewolves. They belong to Dux Bellorum. They are only one group of his many minions. They are all converging here. If you stay, you will have to choose to join either him or me. I think you would prefer me."

"You only say that because you need my help."

She acknowledged him with a slight nod. "I can certainly use your help, but I will get along without it. You need *me*, Ricardo."

"Oh no. I cannot let you have a foothold in the city, Doña Elinor. I am the Master of Santa Fe. I'm declaring myself so right now."

"You can't just declare yourself Master of a city, Ricardo," the Abbot said.

"That's exactly what Elinor said. And well, I didn't know that. I'm still not entirely sure what's involved in becoming Master of a city. I know there's the whole business of challenging and killing an existing Master and draining his or her blood. But surely there was a first Master of the first city. That would have been what—the Master of Uruk? *Was* there a Master vampire of Uruk?"

"It's not generally believed so, no."

"And there must have been a first Master of every city that has a Master. Who decided? They didn't spring into existence when the cities all came into existence, did they? I imagine they are made like the cities themselves. Santa Fe used to be little more than a way station for travelers. The same with Denver, El Paso, in all of them there must have been a point where a vampire arrived and decided they liked it enough to call it theirs, and—why are you looking at me like that?"

The Abbot frowned. Drew an obvious breath to be able to speak. "I thought once I met you, your story would become more clear. It has not."

"I don't understand why this is so difficult. I'm being totally straightforward."

"You are a very badly trained vampire, Ricardo."

He had not been trained at all. "Yes, I've been told that

often. I can't say I mind too much. The well-trained ones haven't impressed me very much."

"No, I suppose not."

"May I continue? I was just getting to the good part."

"Please."

"Do you even know what's involved in declaring yourself Master of a city?" Elinor said, disbelieving. Her minions had put hands on weapons, arranging themselves in a defensive pose in what they thought was a subtle manner.

"Not really," Ricardo said. "And I don't really care. Santa Fe is under my protection now."

"You can't just walk into a city and say that it's yours—"

"Isn't that what you planned on doing? What this Dux Bellorum plans? I was here first! This city is mine!"

"Only for as long as you can hold it," she said. "You can't stay out of the fight, Ricardo. You're too strong."

He tilted his head. "I am?" She flushed, pursed her lips, as if she hadn't meant to say that and wished she could take it back. He gave her half a grin, wry and wicked. "Strong enough to hold Santa Fe, you think?"

"It would be better if we worked together."

"Yes, it would. But then you will be like your Mistress Catalina and demand obedience, and then you and I will fight, and it will all be very messy, and I'd rather not play those games."

She angrily sliced a hand at him. "Those games are what being a vampire is all about."

"I have a confession, Doña Elinor. I think I hate vampires."

She laughed. "There is no arguing with you. Not two hundred years ago, and you haven't changed a bit. Farewell then, Ricardo. If you change your mind, I will always welcome you." Tipping her chin at her minions, she turned to go.

He said, "Elinor. One question: What kills wolf men? These werewolves?"

Her expression when she looked at him made her seem as baffled as she'd yet been. "You don't know? In all this time you've never had to deal with werewolves?"

"I have not."

"And why should I tell you?"

"Because if I manage to drive them off, you will not have to deal with them," he said, and she nodded.

"Silver. Silver blades, silver bullets. Cut the skin with it."

It was a testament to the strangeness of his life that this sounded not just possible but reasonable. "Good. Thank you."

She started to leave again, and one of the other vampires pleaded with her. "But Mistress, if he joins with Dux Bellorum—"

"There is no danger of that, I think. Don Ricardo is his own man."

Then they were gone, and he heaved a sigh. How much he would have liked to sit down with one of these old vampires, hear their stories, learn the histories of how any of them had come to be . . . but they were all so *conniving.*

When he came back to the courtyard, his would-be allies were lined up before him, looking somber but determined. They must have been watching over the low wall, which meant they had some idea of what was about to happen. He ought to lock them all in the house and flee. They would be safer. Most mortals in the city would have no idea what was going on tonight. That would be better. But these people were here, they knew too much, and he had put them in danger.

Then he noticed that Imelda Constance held a small cup filled with blood, and that they all had bandages tied to their forearms.

"What?" Ricardo asked warily.

Imelda stepped forward. She looked like she was offering him communion. The thought horrified him.

She said, "When you would not eat, I asked Juan what you like. I thought I could make you something special that would tempt you. Then he told us all what you need. And so . . ." She held out the cup.

"It's none of your concern, Imelda," Ricardo said, biting the words sharply. "I told him I would take care of it—"

"Juan said if we all gave just a little, it would be enough, and no one would be hurt by it. So we did. This is from all of us." Imelda offered the cup, one of her delicate teacups with roses painted around the edge. The blood was still warm, smelled rich and lovely. Ricardo's throat closed; he wanted to cry.

"Lucinda, in your condition you cannot spare—"

"Oh yes I can." She glared. "Don't you dare coddle me."

"John—"

The Navajo man said, "I don't like it. But if it works?"

"Even you, Padre?"

Father Diego's voice trembled a little but he stood firm when he said, "Juan said . . . he said if you were strong, you really could protect the city. That you have done it before."

159

They would none of them back down. And besides, the blood was already given. They knew he wouldn't be so rude as to waste it once it had been spilled.

He bowed his head. Tried to smile. "This is one of the kindest things anyone has done for me. I have no words."

"Whatever it is that is happening—stop it," Imelda said.

"Win this battle, Conquistador," said John.

Reconciled, he took the cup from Imelda, his chill hand brushing her warm skin, raised the cup in a toast, and drank. After several days without feeding, the blood hit him hard, like whiskey set on fire. His nerves had been growing sluggish, his muscles stiffening. Now they blazed, and the heat grew. His skin flushed with the borrowed blood.

They tasted of fear, all of them. But not the immediate animal fear of prey. This was more uncertain, and with it came fortitude. Power. The will to stand. And there was magic—a spice, a charge like this blood had been touched by lightning. If he had had to guess which of them this spark had come from, he wouldn't have been able to. They all had it. They were all holy, all magical, all powerful.

There must have been something fraught in his gaze when he looked up, because their eyes widened. Diego crossed himself.

Ricardo finished off the last of the blood, then wiped his finger around the inside of the cup and sucked the finger, then sucked every drop from his teeth and tongue. He wouldn't waste a drop of the gift. "Amigos, we have much work to do."

There was declaring himself Master of the city, and then there was making it real. If he only had a bit more time . . . The thought made him laugh. Until now he had had so much more time than he should have. At the moment he had allies, which was just as good.

Father Diego had silver at the church. Chalices, candlesticks, decorations, all of them holy. Ricardo didn't know if that would make them more powerful, but it couldn't hurt. He felt guilty asking the priest to cut up the items, to wake up a metalsmith to melt and mold them into spear points. But he was already damned with his curse, so let the blame fall on him.

John went with Diego. The pair would summon every priest, monk, medicine man, and healer from every church, abbey, mission, and tribal house they could reach, all of them blessing everything they could along the way.

"I can't believe I'm doing this," Father Diego muttered, just before Ricardo saw them off. "'Thou shalt have no other gods before me.' All my own blessings will be undone by the others."

"No, Padre," Ricardo said. "They will be doubled. I'm sure of it."

"And am I to listen to a demon who drinks blood?"

"I'm a Catholic like you, Father. Perhaps not so good a one. But I believe all prayers offered by good people in good faith are strong. Don't you?"

John listened to the conversation politely, then looked to Ricardo to explain. In Apache the vampire said, "Padre Diego doubts any magic but his own."

The Navajo smiled thinly. "So do I. But between all of us, one of our prayers ought to work."

"What did he say?" Diego demanded.

"The more prayers are offered, the more likely one is to work."

The priest's brow furrowed. "That almost makes sense."

"It does, doesn't it? I often find that the case where magic and demons are concerned. Go, look after each other, and be careful."

The pair went into the night. Lucinda and Imelda were next.

"I do not like sending you out into the dark," Ricardo said, sighing at the pair of them.

"Stop being all chivalrous," Lucinda said. "We'll be fine."

Imelda nodded. "We know Santa Fe very well, Don Ricardo. We know just what to do."

"Thank you both so much." He gripped both their hands, overwhelmed. How had he come to be so fortunate in his friends?

"Until we meet again," Lucinda said. Shawls wrapped tightly over their heads and around their shoulders, they quickly went out into the street arm in arm, both of them clinging to the large basket of herbs and talismans that the curandera had provided.

He had one more meeting before he went out to do his own work. Back in the house, he sat by the bed in the sickroom. The chair creaked, and the eyes of the man in the bed cracked open.

"Still here?" Juanito said softly, his breath failing him.

"I'm afraid I've done something foolish," Ricardo said.

"Wouldn't be the first time."

"You remember the story of why I never travel south of El Paso?"

"You angered the demons who live in Ciudad de México. You promised to keep away from them."

"Yes. Well. One of them has come here. And I . . ."

Juanito chuckled. "This is another fight that you didn't start but you plan to finish, yes?"

"Just so."

"I . . . I cannot help you this time, my friend."

"I know. Except for all the times you already have. What would I do without you, Juanito?" Ricardo said, then wished he hadn't. He would go on. And on, and on.

"You have many friends. They will always help you, if you let them," Juanito said, reaching out a shaking hand. Ricardo squeezed it tightly. "Warm," Juanito said, chuckling. "You let them feed you, then. Good."

"I need it, with what I'm about to do."

"Yes."

"I'll come back as soon as I can."

Juanito nodded. His eyes closed. Ricardo watched the worn shirt, waiting for the rise and fall of breathing. And yes, it came, though shallowly. Ricardo must win this battle so that his friend could die in peace, if nothing else.

He found a spear leaning by the courtyard gate, what looked like the handle of a broom with a rough blade of beaten silver strapped to one end. John had already delivered the first of the weapons.

He was no longer exhausted. In fact, he thought he might be able to fly. Spread his arms like wings and let himself float away . . . he had heard stories that some vampires could fly. Perhaps he had to age a few more centuries before gaining that power. Right now, though, he could run. He could taste currents of air around him, the ancient stone mountains to the west, the desert heat from the east, and the hint of blood from the thousands of souls living in the town. If he was very still, he could hear their hearts, follow the pounding of each living drum to his prey—

Now those were not his prey. He watched, listened, tasted the air, and found the musky, distinctive scent of the wolf men. Half skin, half fur; steel and wild. Howls with the hint of human words behind them, or words that might turn into howling. They were all through the city, running and hunting.

He found two of them approaching the plaza. One walked as a man, one as a wolf. The man carried a pistol and a wooden spear. Ricardo held back, admiring the striking image the pair made: a hardened gunman with his oversized wolf companion, who nevertheless gazed with knowing eyes. The wolf was the lookout, ears up, tail straight out, nose working hard. Likely, he could smell vampire. Ricardo stayed downwind. When the pair paused at the intersection between one street and the next, he ran fast.

They might have heard a whistle in the air before they saw him, the wind of his passage, racing faster than anyone ought to be able to. He struck the man first, coming from behind, not really caring about honor and fair fights, not on a night like this. A thin strip of bare neck, white skin, shone between the collar of his coat and the fringe of his hair. Ricardo stabbed here with the silver; his unworldly strength drove the makeshift blade through skin. Blood sprayed. The man cried out and fell to his knees, which surprised Ricardo; the wound wasn't deep. He'd meant to go for the front of his throat, not the back.

The wolf was on Ricardo in the next moment, leaping, jaws closing over the wrist that held his weapon. Teeth tore into his skin; he dropped the silver. Growling, slavering, the wolf used all his weight and claws to shove Ricardo to the ground. Ricardo dug his hands into the creature's fur and heaved. Drawing on all the considerable strength of his borrowed blood, he managed to throw the creature back. The wolf let out a whimper, scuttled back to his feet.

The man groaned in agony, his back arched, reaching for the wound, which trailed black threads through his skin, from his neck across his face. Poison, the silver was poison to them. A moment later he fell still.

Enraged, the wolf came at Ricardo again. Ricardo stood, feet apart, ready for him. He should have been terrified, facing down a charging monster. But he knew he was stronger. And the wolf wasn't thinking clearly. The open jaws came for his throat, and Ricardo stepped aside at the last moment, grabbed the creature by the head, and wrenched until he heard the crack of bone and the wolf's body went limp. He let it fall to the ground, waited a moment.

The wolf whined. Amber eyes blinked back at him, furious and afraid. So, the creatures could be injured. This would heal, in time. Ricardo looked around for the silver knife. The wolf jerked, trying to stand.

"I am sorry," Ricardo said. "But this is war and I have people to protect."

He dug through fur to stab the wolf's throat, while the wolf struggled to let out a choked howl. And then he was still. Ricardo watched a moment, and the wolf transformed in death. The fur vanished, the limbs melted, re-formed, until a human man lay at Ricardo's feet, naked and limp. Too young, with brown skin and dark hair, the start of a beard. And how had such a one come to this? Ricardo whispered a prayer, commending the boy's soul to God.

Wiping the silver with a handkerchief, he went in search of the next enemy.

At the edge of town, he found a trio of vampires harassing a troop of guards on a trading caravan. The vampires were looking to feed and seemed the kind who played with their food, herding them against a wall, knocking their heads, and retreating to shadow while their victims lay stunned. Ricardo didn't know which side these vampires were on, Elinor's or her enemies, but he didn't much care. He came up behind and plunged wooden stakes through their backs, one after the other, before any of them knew what attacked.

These vampires were not old. The old ones turned to ash when they died, the decay of centuries falling on them at once. These merely fell into desiccated corpses, the rot of a couple of decades at most. He didn't say prayers for them.

As he stood over them, their victims gaped, cringing back even as they reached for weapons.

"Buenas noches, señores," he said and ran. The men said later that a ghost had saved them, the spirit of one of the old conquistadors returned to defend the road.

Approaching the plaza, Ricardo went down one street and had to stop abruptly. A force pressed him back, something smoky and distasteful. He tried to continue forward, and the dread building in him made it impossible. It was the same feeling he got when he tried to enter a church; the threshold of it might as well have been a wall.

This ground had been consecrated. Entire streets made holy. Father Diego had been here.

"Thanks be to God," Ricardo murmured and turned back the way he came.

At another street he heard singing, the chanting and drumming of a group of Apache men, a holy song. Ricardo smiled.

On yet another street he found a pair of women lighting little candles in paper lanterns, lining the whole street with them, one every few feet. He arrived in time to see a shadow pacing them, stalking them. Ricardo raced ahead, got between the vampire and his prey, and stabbed him with his stake. The vampire was the young man Ricardo had confronted earlier that night, Elinor's henchman. He looked at Ricardo reproachfully before sliding to the ground, his skin turning gray, dry, and dying.

"I told you to look out for each other," Ricardo said when he returned to Imelda and Lucinda.

"We killed the other one of them who came for us," Lucinda said. "This one was a lot quieter."

"How goes it?" Ricardo asked.

Imelda beamed. "Beautiful, isn't it?"

"Yes, but will it stop them?"

Lucinda's smile was wicked. "Every single one has a prayer. This *will* work."

"Bueno. I must be off."

He ran, tracking more trails of cold, of ill will. He killed four more werewolves and another three vampires, using speed, stealth. Using the fact that none of them seemed to be expecting opposition. At least not opposition like him, a desperate assassin. They had come ready to face an army. He didn't see Elinor and wondered what would happen if he tried to kill her. She might be the one vampire here who was older than he was. Stronger. He didn't know if he could kill her. Perhaps if he left her with no allies, she would negotiate.

This city was his, he was Master here. *This* was how Masters were made.

Soon, he was running out of places he could travel. Holy lights lit whole sections of streets. Father Diego's prayers protected others. The plaza was awash in prayers and spells of protection. All of it raised Ricardo's spirits. He came to an unprotected section and waited, testing the air, listening. Waiting for more opponents to reveal themselves.

But there was nothing. The air was clear, empty, smelling of pine trees and sage, and the heady smell of candles burning. Maybe it was done, over. Maybe they had won.

Then, a lone figure approached, walking in the middle of the street. He appeared Anglo, of average height, clean shaven, a fine-boned face. He was dressed in a duster over a dark wool waistcoat and starched shirt, tailored trousers, polished boots. Neat, finely made. Almost luxurious for all that he seemed straightforward. Ricardo felt grubby by comparison, but then he'd had a rough evening. He only now noticed the spatters of blood across his shirt in addition to the blood from the bullet wound. He waited for the man's approach. The stranger stopped, still some distance away. Close enough to be heard. Close enough to shoot in the eye with a pistol.

"You're Dux Bellorum, of course," Ricardo stated, unsure of himself but faking arrogance.

"No," the man said. "I'm not." He spoke Spanish with a perfect Castilian accent, much like Ricardo's own.

"You are not a vampire. Who are you?"

The Abbot had gone pale as a sheet of parchment, even after drinking blood an hour before.

"What's wrong?" Ricardo said.

"Describe him to me."

"Not quite thirty, I'd guess. Pale skin, young-looking, but hard. Handsome. Black hair. Not tall. Arrogant."

"And his name," the Abbot said, leaning forward, pleading with desperation. "What was this man's name? Did he tell you?" His eyes were wide. Afraid. He had been a vampire for thousands of years, and now he was afraid.

"Let me think a moment, let me remember—" He had not thought of any of this in so long. And now . . . what was wrong? His spine had gone cold. Even colder.

"Ricardo, please! What did he call himself?"

"I'm thinking . . ." Ricardo's eyes widened. He had it.

"I'm not Dux Bellorum," the man said. "I am Carlos de Luz. And you, Ricardo el Conquistador, are a very interesting man."

The name did not reassure the Abbot at all. He gripped the arms of his chair, as if to stop his hands from shaking.

"Lightman," he said. "You saw him. You actually spoke to him."

"Lightman? De Luz—I suppose so. Who is he?"

"Tell the rest of the story. Please. I must hear everything. Don't leave anything out."

"That's what I've been trying to do, but how am I to know what's important and what isn't? How am I supposed to tell the story when you seem so astonished? Why does this old memory terrify you so much?"

"Ricardo!" The Abbot rubbed his face and forced himself to sit back. "*Please.*"

"All right," Ricardo said cautiously and continued.

"What do you want?" Ricardo asked tiredly. He had been prepared to face an army here. To negotiate with either Elinor or this Dux Bellorum character. He was unprepared for . . . whatever this was.

The man looked around, smiling thinly. "A crossroad. I don't always manage these conversations right on a crossroad. But they always seem to go a little better when I do."

Ricardo hadn't noticed, but yes, this was where the main road to the plaza crossed the road to the west and Taos Pueblo. A proper crossroad indeed. "It will be dawn in an hour or so," Ricardo said. "I don't have much time, so whatever conversation you wish to have, make it quick."

"Yes. Of course. I'd like you to come work for me, Ricardo."

"I don't work for anyone, I haven't in a very long time."

"Yes. But I need generals for my war."

Generals. Dux Bellorum. The man Elinor was so wary of was just another soldier. This man held the strings. Did she know that?

"I am not interested in war. I had enough of that a long time ago."

"Even if my war will win you the world?" said de Luz. He seemed serious. His body stood easy, but his face was like stone.

Ricardo laughed. "You seem young, so let me tell you what I have learned: They all say that. Those who make war always promise the world. I don't want it."

"Then what do you want?"

"To be left alone, señor, truly. Why does no one understand this?"

Grinning, he shook his head. "That's not what you want. At least not all of it. Let's try again. What do you want?"

"To not have my patience tried." He started to turn away.

"Let me make you a different offer. I can offer you life. Make you human again."

Ricardo froze. The thought rattled in his skull a moment. Life. Warmth. To make his own blood, his own heat. To see the sun again. To have the life that had been stolen . . . Could de Luz turn back time? Could he send young Ricardo de Avila back to Spain, with everything he knew now so that he could choose differently?

And would he really choose differently? To forget all that he had seen. Everyone that he had met. *God has a plan for me,* he used to tell himself. *God has meant for this to happen.* Inadequate comfort, and these days he was fairly certain God didn't concern himself with the lives of lone naive Spaniards.

"Don Ricardo?" de Luz prompted.

"Who are you that you would have such power? I've never met anyone who could do this thing."

He shrugged. "I'm just someone who makes deals."

"And what price do you ask for this astonishing thing you offer?"

"I'm sure we can come to some kind of arrangement."

Chuckling, Ricardo said, "Oh no, this is the same deal as

the first. I become yours, for you to do with as you see fit. We're back where we started, señor. That life is no life at all. Buenas noches." He started to walk away.

The man called after him. "One last offer, and this is the last. Your friend, Juan. Juanito. He is dying. I can offer him life. Without the price that you have paid. That's why you haven't offered to turn him yourself, yes? You could walk into that house right now and save your best friend's life. But you don't."

"This isn't life, it's a curse."

"Be that as it may. But there are more things in heaven and earth than are dreamt of in your philosophy, as they say."

"I don't doubt that."

"I can offer your friend life. I can heal him."

Ricardo would take nothing for himself. But for Juanito? He clenched his fist. He would give himself to this man to save Juanito. It would be easy.

"What did you tell him?" the Abbot said. "Did you accept his offer? It's very, very important. Did you accept?"

"Why is this so important?" Rick was growing angry.

"Who do you think this man was, Ricardo? What did you think of him, standing there in Santa Fe almost two hundred years ago?"

"I thought he was a trickster. A magician. A con man. He liked theatrics. Maybe he could really help Juanito, maybe he couldn't, but I didn't trust him."

"And what did you say to him, when he made you this offer?"

"Abbot. Who was de Luz?" Ricardo demanded. "Who is Lightman?"

The Abbot's gaze turned to the Scribe. Rick implored the figure at the lectern, who nodded and recited from a work that was not as old as Rick but still told an ancient story, "'. . . what time his pride had cast him out from heav'n, with all his host of rebel angels, by whose aid aspiring to set himself in glory above his peers, he trusted to have equaled the Most High . . .'"

Ricardo blinked. "You can't be serious."

"The War in Heaven never ended," the Abbot said. "We fight it still. So you must tell me by all that is holy on earth and in every realm beyond, when the Devil stood before you at the crossroad and made you an offer, *did you accept?*"

For just a moment, the bottom dropped out of Ricardo's world. The ground tipped, his head swam. It was like learning years later that the ship you were supposed to have been on but weren't sank, killing all on board. Like leaving San Francisco right before the earthquake. He had not known the danger. If he had, it would have destroyed him on the spot.

Then, he laughed. He laughed so hard he doubled over a cramping stomach and fell out of the chair. He settled on the floor, wiping tears streaming from his eyes. And then he lifted his gaze to the soaring ceiling and gave thanks to God.

"What's so funny?" the Abbot asked. "This is serious." The Scribe stared, even through the blindfold. The pen was still.

"Abbot. Don't you understand what this means? This . . . this is *wonderful.*"

"I don't understand."

Rick leaned back against the screen, stretched out his legs. He felt drunk. He felt amazing. He pointed at the Abbot. "You're telling me I stood on the crossroads with the Devil, who offered to make me a deal. What does the Devil trade in? What would I sell to take his offer?"

"Your soul."

He slapped the stone floor. "Which means I still have one. I still have my soul, and God still listens to me. My prayers are still good. For centuries everyone has tried to tell me I have no soul, that being made a vampire destroyed my soul. And yet the Devil stood there trying to buy it." He laughed again. "I have my soul!"

The Abbot stared. "Then you told him no?"

Rick sighed. He'd been gasping, to take in enough air for that laugh. He was wrung out and high, all at the same time. "Yes, Abbot. I told him no. Praise be to God."

Ricardo could give away himself to save Juanito—and Juanito would not thank him for it. Juanito would never speak to him again, in fact. Perhaps . . . perhaps he should leave his friend's fate to God. Maybe a better life really did await him.

"No," Ricardo said softly.

"No?" De Luz stared at him. "No? Just like that?"

"Just like that. I know better than anyone that death is not the end. Adios, Señor de Luz. I have things I must attend to."

"You're just one man," de Luz said. Ricardo kept walking. "Someone else will use you as a pawn. Someday you won't be able to walk away!"

Ricardo waved over his shoulder and turned the corner. Not sure where else he ought to go, he headed back to Imelda's house. In fact, this was the only way he could go. The whole city was protected, its streets consecrated with burning incense, tin milagros nailed on doors and gates, Zuni fetish carvings, paintings made with sand, a dozen other various totems and charms from a dozen different traditions. Voices in several languages were singing in the plaza, clashing with one another but at this distance sounding like a dream. No sounds of battle at all.

Elinor was waiting at the gate to the courtyard, leaning on the wall, her arms crossed, a wry look on her face. Like she had no opinion on the matter of the night's events.

"I was wondering when I'd see you again," Ricardo said. "How are you?"

"I can't get into Santa Fe. I don't know what you did, but it worked."

"I told you, I am Master here." He winked. "If it's any consolation, your enemy cannot enter the town either."

"I suppose it'll have to be. What did you do?"

"I asked for help. Elinor—" He didn't know quite how to warn her. With the sky turning gray, the light of dawn tugging at him, he wasn't sure the encounter had even happened. "I don't know anything about this Dux Bellorum, and I hope not to. But you should know that he isn't alone. There are other powers around him. I don't like it."

"Well, one villain at a time, I think. Goodbye, Ricardo. I must go report what happened here. One way or another . . ."

"What will you tell your Mistress about me?"

She shook her head wryly. "I will not tell anyone anything. They will not believe me. But at least now you will stay in one place for a while, and I will know where to find you."

Ricardo wasn't sure about that. He could call himself Master, but . . . he wasn't sure that Santa Fe needed one, not after tonight. His travels beckoned. "I don't know. I have stopped trying to predict anything."

"You could be a king. Do you realize how much power you've gathered?"

He did not. He did not want to know. "The kings all seem to have so much to worry about."

"Good night." She tossed a haphazard bow, took a step—and then ran, with a burst of speed that turned her into shadow. She was gone. He went into the house, to Juanito's room.

They were all there—Imelda, Lucinda, John, and Father Diego—each praying in his or her own way, hands clasped and heads bent. And Juanito lay on the bed, too still, too cold. Ricardo was too late; he'd missed it. Dead, the man looked twenty years older, his flesh hanging in folds, gray and lifeless. His hair seemed to have become translucent. Sleeping eyes had movement to them, the hint of dreaming. But he was so, so still. Sunken into the blankets. Dead.

De Luz. De Luz had killed him, when Ricardo refused his offer—

No. This had been coming for days. Slowly, he came to the side of the bed, knelt down, and rested his elbows on the mattress, put his face in his hands. *I'm sorry, I'm sorry, Juan. I cannot save anyone.*

A hand touched his shoulder, a gentle pressure. Imelda. Ricardo clasped it, grateful for the contact. Her skin was burning compared to his, as cold as Juan's. As dead as he was.

"His passing was easy," she said softly. "He went to sleep and sighed, and God carried him away."

Ricardo would miss him. As he missed everyone, all the way back to Suerte and his family right at the start. He carried them all with him, and the weight was heavy.

"I think . . . I am very tired and must sleep. We . . . we can take care of him in the evening. Father, can you—"

"Yes, I will make arrangements," Diego said.

"Thank you all," he said to each of them. "Thank you all so much for your . . . your faith." They each nodded back to him in turn. Ricardo took a blanket off the back of a nearby chair, wrapped it over his shoulders. "If you could close the door on the way out and not let anyone back in until dusk, I would be most grateful."

"Señor—" Lucinda said. They all looked back at him, worried.

He didn't have the strength to do more than smile and nod. He got down on the floor, crept under the bed, wrapped the blanket all around him, and then dawn dragged him into the sleep of the dead.

"And that's everything?" the Abbot asked.

"I don't know, is it? What else do you want to know? I stayed in Santa Fe a month, making sure that the protections held, that Elinor or the werewolves didn't return. It was never really my city though, Abbot. After, I rode to Bent's Fort as we had planned. Found my next job as a guide. Made do as best I could, as I had for decades. When is my next appearance in your great book?" He turned to the Scribe.

"Virginia City, 1860."

"Ah yes," Rick said. "The Comstock Lode. It turns out that some packs of werewolves are capable of holding grudges for many years, and a town in the middle of a silver rush is a good place to hide from them."

The Abbot rubbed his face as if he was very tired. "Of course it is."

"I ran a saloon there. The Bucket of Blood Saloon." He chuckled. Ladora had actually owned the saloon. He only helped. She had been tough and lively and wonderful . . . he remembered her, too.

"Of course you did."

"Is there anything else, Abbot?"

Now the Abbot laughed. It started as a quiet chuckle in his gut, until his whole body shook, though he made little sound.

"I cannot believe it. Any of it. Ricardo, you are a vampire, a demon, a monster who drinks blood, and you are so good of heart that you met the Devil on the crossroad and didn't even know it was him."

To be fair, Rick had been distracted at the time. He hadn't thought he was worth the Devil's time.

"And then you turned him down?" The Abbot shook his head. "I didn't believe it. Until I actually met you, I didn't believe it. But here you are."

"I have a number of friends who would also think this was funny."

"See? You have friends. You have had friends for five hundred years. You're not supposed to have friends! You're supposed to have servants and thralls! You're a vampire, and you have the gall to have *friends*?"

He would not have survived without his many, many friends. He felt their ghosts line up behind him.

"I have never been very good at being a vampire," he said.

"On the contrary, I think you may be the best of us. And now . . . and now we need you."

"He's still out there, isn't he?" Rick said. "I know Dux Bellorum is. But de Luz holds his leash. They're planning."

"They've been planning for two thousand years, and now it's all come to a head. We need you, Ricardo el Conquistador."

"You are making me an offer?"

"No, I am asking for your help. Which I think is something you understand. Here at the Order of Saint Lazarus of the Shadows, we are vampires who are determined to serve God, whether He wants our service or not. And you . . . you have just proven that we still have souls to salvage. Will you join us, Ricardo, you who have never joined anyone in all your years?"

He had spent so much time fleeing, hiding. Then he thought that Denver, one small city, easily overlooked against the backdrop of the world, would be enough. Some small power to keep the people he cared about safe.

He had a friend—strange enough for one like him, as the Abbot had already said—who was a werewolf—even stranger, the old man would say if he knew, but surely he knew about Katherine, the werewolf called Kitty, who had already stepped in the light of the world to use what small power she had to protect her own. And anyone else she

179

could manage to save, in the end. What would she say, if she were here? Besides demanding to know how old the Abbot really was. Ricardo el Conquistador thought she would say—take the step.

Rick nodded. "I would like to face de Luz again. To thank the Devil for showing me my soul."

AUTHOR'S NOTE

There was a time when I was absolutely certain I had no interest in writing about vampires. *Everybody* wrote about vampires. They were everywhere, always. The clichés had clichés. I didn't need to add to that mess, I had nothing new to say about them. So when I started writing stories about a talk radio advice show for supernatural creatures, I made my main character a werewolf named Kitty because I was pretty sure no one had done that before. Early on, I mostly included vampires in that world so I could make fun of them.

That didn't last long. Vampires eventually draw an aura of gravitas around them. They start to fill up the room. You can't not take them seriously. Their eyes are hypnotic.

Almost from the moment I knew Rick had traveled with Coronado's expedition when he was a young man, I also knew I would have to start filling in his five hundred years of history between then and the time of the Kitty novels, in which Rick is a major player. And that was when I discovered that I did have something to say about vampires, and I did have an interest in writing about them. In a word, it's the history.

The blood, the power, the seduction, the sex and twisted romance and all the rest that seems to be so ingrained in the modern vampire mythos? Not really interested. But give me a character who has lived for five hundred, eight hundred, a thousand, five thousand years—I will write about all that history in a flaming undead heartbeat.

In giving Rick this particular backstory, which I did because it sounded cool at the time, I inadvertently made him a witness to the entire history of European colonization and settlement of the American West. This is a region with an extraordinary history and character that gave rise to its own genre of film and literature. Its own mythology. Rick is in the middle of it all, and the potential for story is vast. Rick gave me the idea of the vampire as an embodiment of history. Rick takes all that history personally.

A lot of the short stories I write set in the world of the Kitty novels are origin stories for the other characters. I wanted to have those stories established in my own mind, even if they never made their way into Kitty's story. That I can share them with readers and give them some insight is a bonus. "Conquistador de la Noche" is Rick's origin story. "Hidalgo de la Noche" is almost a second origin story, as he moves to the next part of his life, from Colonial Mexico to the Borderlands, where he spends most of the next few hundred years. The challenge in writing this story was doing the research: there's a massive amount of information available to a nonacademic enthusiast (whose Spanish is just barely good enough to order food and complain about the weather) about the conquistador period of Rick's first story, and there's a ton of information about the missionary period, when Spanish settlement, much of it driven by evangelizing Catholic priests, moved north into the Southwest and Rocky Mountain regions of what is now the United States. But there's about a hundred years in between those two periods where I couldn't find much information at all. This is the challenge of writing historical fiction: sometimes you just have to wing it. The important thing here is that one of Rick's primary survival strategies is making friends. He didn't know he wasn't supposed to.

In *Kitty Raises Hell*, the sixth novel of the series, I drop a hint that during his travels, Rick once met Doc Holliday, the famous gunman and gambler. It's a throwaway line meant to annoy Kitty, because Rick won't tell Kitty the story. (Rick hasn't told Kitty *any* of these stories.) Let this be a lesson to writers everywhere: If you add a throwaway line because you think it sounds cool, at some point you may have to write an entire story explaining it.

The sections of this book that are new, Rick coming to Rome and telling his story to the Abbot of the Order of Saint Lazarus of the Shadows, take place after the events of *Kitty Rocks the House*, when Father Columban comes to Denver to recruit Rick into the Order. This sets the stage for the final book in the series, *Kitty Saves the World*, when Carlos de Luz, aka Charles Lightman, aka a dozen other names, appears again.

The new story, covering the events of 1848, also incorporates the fact that every time I drive through New Mexico, which is usually several times a year, I think about Rick and what he might have been doing during his couple of hundred years of traveling in this region. I once stood in the

Plaza of Santa Fe, on the street outside the cathedral, and had this visceral jolt that traveled through my feet and all my nerves: Ricardo de Avila stood right on that very spot. He's a fictional character, but he was there, I just knew it, without a doubt. And so I wrote about it.

I have been writing stories about Kitty, Rick, and their world for twenty years now. That I still find so much to write about here is a wonder and a joy. That so many readers are interested in that world is a blessing. Thank you for reading.

ABOUT THE AUTHOR

Carrie Vaughn is the *New York Times* best-selling author best known for her Kitty Norville urban fantasy series. The series, about a werewolf who hosts a talk radio advice show for supernatural beings, includes fourteen novels and a collection of short stories.

Vaughn is also the author of the superhero novels in the Golden Age saga and has been a regular contributor to the Wild Cards shared-world novels edited by George R. R. Martin. In addition, Vaughn writes the Harry and Marlowe steampunk short stories featuring alien technology in an alternate nineteenth-century setting.

Vaughn received the 2018 Philip K. Dick Award for her novel *Bannerless.* She is also the winner of the RT Reviewer Choice Award for Best First Mystery for *Kitty and the Midnight Hour* and the WSFA Small Press Award for best short story for "Amaryllis." She has a master's degree in English literature, graduated from the Odyssey Fantasy Writing Workshop in 1998, and returned to the workshop as writer in residence in 2009.

A bona fide air force brat (her father served on a B-52 flight crew during the Vietnam War), Vaughn grew up all over the U.S. but managed to put down roots in the area of Boulder, Colorado, where she pursues an endlessly growing list of hobbies and enjoys the outdoors as much as she can. She is fiercely guarded by a miniature American Eskimo dog named Lily.